whiteheart:
prologue to hysteria

by Lesego Rampolokeng

poetry
horns for hondo (cosaw, fordsburg) 1990
talking rain (cosaw, fordsburg) 1993
end-beginnings (marino verlag, munchen) 1998
blue v's (with cd) (editions solitude, stuttgart) 1998
the bavino sermons (gecko, durban) 1999
the second chapter (pantolea press, berlin) 2003

recordings
end-beginnings (shifty, johannesburg) 1992
end-beginnings (recrec, london) 1993
the HALF ranthology (mehlo-maya, johannesburg) 2002

play
fanon's children (mehlo-maya, johannesburg) 2002

novel
blackheart (pine slopes, johannesburg) 2004

whiteheart:
prologue to hysteria

lesego rampolokeng

ISBN: 0-9584542-3-x

deep south
p.o. box 6082
grahamstown
6140
www.deepsouth.co.za
contact@deepsouth.co.za

We gratefully acknowledge financial assistance for publishing this book from
The National Arts Council

deep south titles are distributed by
University of KwaZulu-Natal Press
www.ukznpress.co.za
books@ukzn.ac.za

Cover painting : Lauren Shear
Cover and text design : Paul Wessels
Layout : Martin Hiller

for ous lala

i got out of it in a haze, a mist both whirling outside me and
in. i blinked in the sun. i stopped from a stagger & sat down
hard in a mud patch. the walls closed me in. out of them.
it was then and now a transitional phase. it is personal, it
was national. i woke out of it like a dream, euphoria swirling
around and in. only it had taken disillusionment to get me
back to reality or what i had been made to see as it. the
doors closed behind my time and now open on that which
was made unmine.

i heard a sickening crack of bone and saw the blow split my
mother's lip and throw her against the wall. he had a grin on
his face as he advanced. in the next room my sister screamed
the walls down. it came down hard inside my head. trying
to break out. my mother was not crying anymore. the walls
were. red as the sun crashed down through the torn curtains.
he kicked her in the stomach & i saw her body heave itself
off the weeping wall and crash out through her mouth.
his mouth twisted to the side in disgust. it was a mass of
twitches when the smell of vomit clung to the air. i was not
crying anymore. i heard her say she loved him. my mother's
pupils rolled out of sight. it was pain when she slithered
down. slowly. softly. i thought i heard the rain come down
hard beyond the walls. but it wasn't. he was a big man, &
us? we were so small. all of us. i heard the walls crack. those
blows slashing into my mother's flesh opened holes in my
soul i'm still trying to close. i started to run towards mama
& a huge boot rushed at me. my neck was liquid heat when
i spun around. i felt the wall knock against the back of my
head as i grabbed empty air. i always do. when he rips into
me in the nights of torture i open my mouth to scream but
it hits against my chest & goes down to where he's heaving
& swearing through his clenched teeth. & his breath creeps
against the nape of my neck.

later we walked for a long time. my sister moaned on my
mother's back. the many times we had walked like that
followed behind us. no, they lead the way. we have been
walking for most of my life. we heard gunshots in the
distance & a scream. lonesome. so tired. my mother's hand

clutched mine. tight. i looked up in the dark.

mother your face cracks against my every minute. when
hunger's heat grows i go out to the abattoir to scavenge
for the skins they tear off the chickens & throw out. bring
them to mama & she goes to the market & comes back with
tomato & onion that's not too bad to cook & we have a great
meal. at times the workers at these places are full of shit. i
was kicked by one when i was crawling around hunting for
some stray skins but someone held me back when i wanted
to slice him like he did the chickens. jesus, those chickens
kick & struggle & the blood spurts & writes on the wall
their obituary. but it's fine when i close my eyes shut them
tight against their cries & last pleas & then battles for their
lives bite into the skins. i hate the sight of raw meat i can't
pass the butchery without the phlegm hitting against my
throat, hard trying to get out & i have to get on my knees &
ask it please don't. it's not the same when they're cooked,
especially fried. but i wonder about hell, often.

the mist rises. clouds form. their strata cracking separating
then reforming. the sounds split open & fold back. in my
mind things crash collide & sink to the bottom of the morass
in my head. ah the stench of it, the decayed days. runny
sores on the face of my memory. i stare at it through my
rheumy eyes. see the day he was hitting mother again & i
swore at him & he came at me & i ran. he reached out to
grab me but i was halfway out of the door slamming it shut
behind me & his hand got caught in the jamb. i turned &
threw everything i had in my system against that door &
stayed there while on the otherside his shrieks his screams
his groans howls sought to break through the wood & i
kept pressing. i pushed against that door & i could feel the
tiny muscles knot on my back tear through my shoulders
& pound against my temples. then i heard the bones crack
& the sound bounced against the walls. & i became aware
from a long way off of my mother first hurling threats then
implorations pleas begging me to let go of the door. when she
started crying i stepped away from the door. i ran out into the
streets. an alley cat. no, gutter rat.

this teacher hated me. she said so to me every day. &
showed it in the straps & sticks & hosepipe coming down
on my head on my back. she hit me with her fists threw
her shoes at me kicked me. it was an everyday thing. it ate
into my brains & i couldn't get anything right. my existence
was wrong. & everything else stemmed from that. when she
wanted the plural for child i said in a real loud proud voice,
because it was so easy, "childs". she said my head was so
big because it was filled with water & the other children
laughed until it bounced from wall to wall off my head & i
wanted to stop it so much i lashed out at the one nearest
me & two of his buck-teeth that looked like they were going
doggies in his mouth jumped out. & then the lashes came
down again. & again. when i tried to run out the silly little
piglets rushed me & lifted me high in the air & back where
she told them to drop me & they did, hard. & i crashed my
head.

but school had to come out & i ran & kept running. & started
running things out of class in the streets. getting reality street
corner knowledge. i made friends with the freaks in the
backstreets. the ones who never saw the sun rise or set. the
people in eternal twilight times. there was glue & benzene. i
took one sniff it hit me in the chest & brought all the pain to
the surface.

i couldn't take another so i left that. my friends were the
retarded ones. & the slow ones. one with a runny nose all
day & night every season. another was short, almost a midget
with very long limbs. they would have called him baboon if
they were not so scared of him. he knew how to beat people
up. his arms would grab a boy from a long distance away
pull him back for a long steady wallop if he was trying to
be a shit. i was a magic footed shebeen dancer. spinning
around twirling pulling the dance from heaven right into the
grave & getting money from the patrons for it. of their own
accord, sometimes not. sometimes when that didn't work i'd
dance & my friends would work the drunken ones' pockets.
often flesh would come apart & we'd run off to another
hunting pit. there was stonefighting in the street & i had an

okapi knife i scraped against the tar in the street & people
applauded clapping & shouting my name. we were fighting
some boys from up the street. these were grown-ups egging
us on. i stabbed a boy in his chest & he lay there. my boys
kicked punched & stoned him. he had broken a bottle in
my girl's face & her cries had made me go dig out the old
knife. & then an elderly man came walking down the street
& someone threw a brick in his face. i think by mistake. it
broke his spectacles right in his face. he screamed & it was
terrible to see the old man clawing at his eyes trying to get
the slivers & bits of bottle out. he fell to his knees shouting
out god's name & the angels. & there was a lot of blood
there. but still i scraped the knife across the street & made
sparks fly right there & the people laughed when i stabbed
the boy & blood flew & i was the star of the show. but
someone's child's dying out there & it's cold mama out here.

when they came in shiny buttons & boots to herd me to
the kraal the girl was trembling in the back of the van &
we held hands while they guffawed & told us to fuck while
they watched. one said he'd fuck me up the arse with a
baton if we didn't. we just trembled against each other &
collided heavily when the van hit speed-bumps. it seemed
to be laughing from deep in its belly too. two of them were
watching us with their zippers bursting under the strain of
minds struggling against vile thought. at the police station
they had me chained to a bench & made the flesh jump off
my back for hours while they sat around laughing telling me
i would grow up to become a psychopath. when i bled one
brought a salt shaker shook it above the welt & the pain
jumped deep into my head. when the girl screamed they
hollered even louder. it went on for ever until they led the girl
to some dark corner down the ringing corridors. i could hear
her moans. still do. coming down the passages of my mind.
but they let us go into the street later that weeping night. into
the rain. in the light i saw the goo slide down her legs & my
shirt was torn hanging around in pieces reaching my ankles. i
knew love & hate at the same time.

we propped each other up. in the snatches of light she

was smiling & the rain washed the blood off my back. it must have washed the dirt off her legs too. but the dirt was somewhere else & it was causing me pain. i screamed alone in the deep night engulfing me with tentacles around my neck. trying to scratch it off my skin. but the agony of it was buried too deep for water to cleanse. she held me close & the stench swung around & went deep inside. the smell of it is still inside me. it creeps out turns and impales me on the lance of its sight deep in the night. always. she told me in the rain about how when she woke up to boys after her father had introduced her to what they had between their legs he went murderous enraged one howling night, called her things she'd heard on filth street grabbed her & sat her down on the hot stove & she burnt. she cried & screamed & the smell of her flesh hung in the air & came down harder than the rain & he held her there. she says she sizzled there & there was juice raining draining from her body. & the walls came crushing down on her senses & she pleaded begged & prayed & the more she tried to wriggle off the stove the more she got burnt in other places than her buttocks & she felt the fire shooting up her vàgina. slicing across memory time & place. she woke up outside with a dog sniffing at her charred genitals. when she was tearing herself up he called her unruly & double fisted the side of her head & she thought her skull came down to sit with her on that hell's stove & she was roast beef. with pieces of steak in the pan frying. i'd seen her body & at first i was afraid to touch her. she trembled making my nerves shudder & pull against my skin & i held her tighter than anytime else. & her smile in the pressing dark pierced its way into my being. she walked on spindly little legs into my history. i did too.

my mother scraped asked & begged & did what not & took me to a sangoma. the healer had flames in her eyes & the smell in her little room full of bones & dark bottles & herbs & animal skins sat down heavily on my stomach. with a dirty rusty razor she made incisions on my elbows forehead chest & ankles. she rubbed snuff mixed with something other in the little wounds. i drank litres of water plus some other medicine on her order stuck two fingers deep in my mouth &

vomited. she saw stories of early death & foreboding times for
me in my vomit. somewhat perversely the tension rose past
hormonal riot level. it was a weird version of sexual frenzy.
she was hissing orgasmic. wriggling her body on the reed-
mat first slowly then accelerating as possession took over her
torso. she gyrated her waist gritting her teeth as snakelike
sounds burst out between her lips.

it hit my groin & i felt it ache as it struggled to rise &
burst through my pants. she was moving like she had a
psychopathic vibrator going up her. at the height of it she
slumped on her buttocks. there was lots of perspiration
on that body after the spirits had left her. she looked at
me glazed, the moon in her eyes. she looked at me a long
time & i flinched, feeling a bit like one receiving peeping
tom attention. like the object of some lewd fantasies. but
somehow i felt it went beyond my pathetic being. it was
copulation with forces much higher & deeper than me & what
hung between my legs. i crossed quickly to hide my erection.

she mixed some more medicines & intoned in a scary
voice straight from the gods calling on my & her ancestors
to merge & take hands in working towards my salvation.
growling all the while invoking the spirits. i almost suffocated
emerged gasping from deep covers of blankets placed over
me hunched above a boiling pot of water & herbs of smells
knocking the breath out of me. they call it steaming. when
i choked she said that was evil spirits throttled deep in
my throat. when she smeared me with animal fat i almost
spilled my load right there in her hands. she covered me
in the medicine from head to foot & i couldn't hide my
condition from her. the experience was sucking my brains
through my toes. she was blind to it but a clouded smile
hovered around her mouth & i felt i was slipping inside my
cranium swimming in grey matter. when they slaughtered
two chickens & smeared the blood over me i didn't lose
consciousness. but i have been doing so ever since. sisters in
the street give the education of life. inductions to the living.
"it's not about whipping it in & wiggling it a bit & whipping
out & wiping it. it's about getting whipped by the flow."

that periods are not a place you go to. found out squirmish
rummaging around in menstrual flood behind the garbage
dump. that cycle drew circles of red around my little member.

i'm always taking girls off into the long grass & the toilets
& sticking my penis inside them. like this one here, she's
always getting boys to go with her. always running her hands
on their pants-front i think she's a little weird. & she's a
montage of burn marks. especially around her vagina. that
i think is what excites about her. these days i can't look at
human deformities. people say her father made her like that.
they hear her scream in her home way into the next street's
night. he's the old man whose spectacles we broke. maybe
that's ok then. but once i was deep inside the girl when i felt
a cold metal object poke into my ribs. i looked up into the
smiling faces of some boys i was sweet with. but they were
not being nice, told me to get finished so they could have a
go. i tried to talk to them but one kicked me in the face & it
threw me off. they had me pinned down with a knife at my
neck while they took turns. five of them. she had an insane
grin on her face throughout. i heard later when she'd grown
up a bit she killed her near blind father & was taken to the
mental asylum. but i didn't see her there when i went.

the father was epileptic. & as was the fashion he was
always creeping into her. rushing jumping her all the way
into her teenage years. so this day he was in the deep end
pumping away for oil. surfing in flesh. when at the height of
his sweating heaving stormtoss, the moment of his orgasm
the highest point of her cries he started doing the electric
boogie. she thought at first he was in particularly intense
coming mode. but then she got terrified scared to shredded
nerves. realizing he'd conked cold out on top of her. all the
while gushing out thrashing about inside her. way up inside
her folds. it was like he was impaling her there & getting
himself planted buried there. his tongue was hanging out
much further than usual. worse than the sight of a salivating
exhausted dog drooling out onto the dust. his saliva was
running down her breasts. it fell like liquid iron on her naked
flesh. was worse than electrodes exploding inside her skull.

some live wire ends came together. she was wearing a
desertstorm weathered smile as he stopped moving after a
time & she rolled him off. loglike. or dead meat. it was off
with his head time. she went out to the kitchen & hefted the
axe in her hands. juggling it about to get the full weight of it
pinned down. then she chopped away. & bits of bone flew all
over the scene. & the rest of it. the blood the gore the brain
torn ligament. times she had to brace herself, throw her build
behind the wooden handle & heave to get it out when it got
stuck so deep it was hard getting it out. & the perspiration
rushed out & dropped amid the mess. much of it we have
seen already, stepped over it & kept walking without a glance
over the shoulder. walking to far sunsets. us born at world's
end.

she couldn't stop chopping away at him. couldn't break him
down to finer particles. she said later she wanted to get to
the core of his dirt. to smash the essence of his being. to
touch the heat of his evil. but she couldn't find it. she got a
knife & sliced him up into strips & strings of meat hanging
there. she wanted to suspend him from the clothesline to air.
to get the stench of the THING out of his flesh. this was her
father it couldn't be him who'd done her bad like that. but he
was so big. she pulled at his innards & skidded on the gore
slippery floor & landed on her buttocks. she wanted to tie his
intestines around his neck but the neck was no longer there.
he was still so heavy. she felt him weighing down on her
body digging in trying to hit & pierce the soul. she couldn't
throw him off. someone said how can you scream without
a throat. so she gave up the idea of dragging him out into
the yard before it was born. she got a hammer & pounded.
trying to hem him into the ground. & the pieces couldn't get
squashed enough. she couldn't get him out of sight. a rat
peeped out of a hole in the wall, grinning, making noises that
struck to the back of her feeling & advanced. she threw the
hammer at it missed as it slithered cowardly back into the
dark hole. this was her father. he wasn't going to be devoured
by filthy creatures.

she stood for a while heaving with the exertion & utter
revulsion of it. then it settled on her mind when it started
itching around where her flesh had been scorched &
mutilated the most. & she remembered. the stove. &
decided to cook him. she got the stove hot & tried twisting
& turning the knobs to get it hottest. even beyond its limits.
but it wouldn't get to the hades heat she wanted. & then
she stewed him. with seasoning & oil & all sorts of goodie
cooking matter. salt & pepper. she cooked the genitals in
a different pot because she relished them the most. the
rest went into a big pot. she was stirring away & shuffling
around with the kitchen steaming while she was singing in
the kitchen constantly threatening to throw her down in all
that fluid. gathering the paprika the black pepper the white
pepper the barbecue spices the garlic & ginger. working away
like the cook she'd been since early childhood for a long time
while the neighbours drawn by the foul stench of it all came
pounding on the doors. but they hadn't done that when he'd
been causing her pain. they knocked shouted & then broke
down the door to find her laughing & crying aloud into the
night. it hasn't dawned yet. she's in the mental asylum. i
was there. they call it a centre for the rehabilitation of the
mentally handicapped. she's no mental cripple. disturbed
they call it at times. but it goes beyond mere disturbance for
me. way away & beyond even an upheaval. it's more than
one long eternal psychological explosion at work on that
human system. it goes deeper than any psychiatry textbook
will ever delve to explore.

but still the street kept running its blades into all of us. one
of the boys died under a flood of lead bricks & bottles. i
don't know if mine was the one that did it. it was about that
time though that once with a girl i felt the vein holding my
foreskin tight to the head go ripping wild & tear. there was
pain there. lots of it & blood flowed staining my pain. in a
few days there was something like cauliflower growing on my
penis. it drove me almost out of my head. mama dragged me
off to hospital & the nurses were bad swearing at me saying
what dirty children were growing up in the townships with
little whores pus dripping from their cunts & little teeth biting

off their cocks & such like things. they gave me a massive injection & tablets & threw me out promising to beat me up if i showed my face there again. i did, several times. in the street they said if you tried doing it with people of other races worse could happen to you than anything else in existence. they said stick to your own & all you'll catch is some yellow smelly liquid running out of your dingaling that's called clap like your penis rises to hit you in the face & laugh. but the pain comes from deep within deeper than your stomach even. they say it pulls at your genitals until you feel you have metal bubbling up between your legs & you walk funny. or else you get bitten a little bit by the small teeth some dirty girls have in their vaginas. they call such girls piranhas or jaws after the film with the murderous shark. but that's nothing. that kind of thing there was medicine for, you know. you could go to the sangoma & get what is called a "pot" to get your machine cleaned up. that would service your engine quick-time. & it was no problem at all. all they did at the sangoma's was give you some luke-warm water, say a bucketful or so, in which some extra strong killer medicine was mixed in. now that concoction was enough to cut off the throat of your little disease. & aside from the taste there was absolutely no come-back from the taking of it. the sangoma would make you drink it, put two fingers way deep into your mouth, jiggle that little thingikie that hangs from the roof of your mouth right at the back & you'd vomit all that filth the girl had given you out. & you'd be able to see it too. wriggling around at the bottom of the bucket or washbasin you'd thrown up, or down, into. you could kick it around if you wanted to. with medicine they give you at the clinic, the thing disappeared & you couldn't tell where it went. well, they knew in the street. it just ran back deep inside you & stayed there for the rest of your life. every now & then popping its head out to chew away at your system & eating up all your children while they were still inside you & running right back before you could do anything about it. but the "pot", jeepers creepers mandela's slippers, the pot killed it there in front of you & your penis' eyes. & all that evil stuff would scream off into the sewerage system when you flushed & you'd walk away laughing, not groaning, into the grave.

or maybe the sangoma would give you an enema. i know
about that because i used to go walking around trying to buy
some dagga at the single sex hostel. that was a while ago
before... well, that's another story altogether. one of burning
pokers in my back as i screamed in one of the rooms. & they
had me on the floor begging them to show mercy & they
called me son of a diseased female dog. & kept feeding the
pokers into the red flames & when one was red haul it out &
stick it into my twelve year old flesh again until i couldn't feel
the pain anymore & woke up outside in the dark & the rain
coming down hard opening up all the vaults to my memories.
but anyway, over weekends especially, i would see rows upon
queues upon lines of naked men standing around in the
communal showers that had no doors to them, with these
plastic containers shaped at one end like a bowl, a kind of
dishthing hanging from a hook in the wall. filled with what
i got to know was herbal medicine & water. these plastic
thingies had tubes leading from the bowl down to a tapering
end shaped much like a penis. & the men would adopt a
pose like they were doing the doggies & with one hand part
the buttocks while with the other insert the penis-shaped end
up the rectum. then with a smart twist of the handle, that
is a little way from the end stuck up the arse, let the liquid
rush from the bowl into the stomach. & moan a little like a
domestic animal being stroked/caressed. & shift & shuffle
around for a while waiting for the stuff to settle. & then
when it was virtually streaming out from between the legs
rush either to the toilet if it wasn't in use or run to the field
opposite dig in the heels & let the shit flow. then walk away
with a smile of utter fulfillment. utter relief. complete purity.
this was how you cleansed your system. no disease could
beat that. not one. especially not one you picked up from
some rotten little whore. no no no. but that was only if it was
a black thing you'd been chewing.

they tell a sorry tale of a boy from down the road who
worked for a white woman as a garden-boy. & every day
she'd sit there while he was trying to do an honest day's
work. concentrating on the serious business of pulling vile
weeds out. or watering the thirsty little flowers. everyday she

sat there with her thighs opened up to heaven. hell, rather.
showing a whole meatloaf of pink down there. he was scared
to look of course. you've heard how white men castrate &
kill you if you take a dive inside that crocodile infested lake.
but you know how black eyes are sharp & can cut through
anything. so what's a look from the corner of the eyes? but
she knew he was looking & wanted it that way. she put
on a whole skin party for him. scratching around in there
round & round & pull her fingers out dripping with juice &
all the while her mouth would be open so he could see right
down the throat i swear. see her liver jumping up & down
in excitement. & it would be so swollen he thought it would
burst. or at least split right down the middle & run to the
pool to cool off.

he'd see her scratching around in there round & up & down
& his fear would reach his crotch. & he'd try keeping his legs
crossed but she'd order him not to. & she'd start moaning
after a while & jerking & thrashing around & making noises
like she was sick. & the boy would be scared spermless &
want to rush over to help but realise seconds later she was
alright when he saw the little smile on her mouth. they say
it happened a number of times just like that but then she
moved on another step & ordered him to drop his pants &
come into her right there on the grass he'd just mowed. but
he'd be scared because she looked so pale he thought he'd
kill her with just one solid sticking. but when it happened
she'd grab him pull him in even deeper than he'd ever gone
with the girls in the ghetto & make worse noises than before
& he didn't know what to do. but then later she'd look at
him in such an ugly way & tell him he was dogshit & things.
but then give him a chunk of bread smeared with red jam
on both sides & an enamel mugful of tea & have him eat
his lunch & go back to working. they say it worked out this
way until late at pitiless night & in his home his parents
heard him scream like he had a knife deep inside him in the
toilet. they broke down the door to find him facing the toilet
bowl with his dick throbbing alive expanding & contracting
standing like he was pissing. which he was. but no urine
ran out of him it was a fluid like they had never seen. sickly

purple-green they said. & as it flowed out so he cried & it
was his life streaming away. & they rushed closer & there
right in the middle of it & inside the toilet bowl letting out a
most foul stench of harbours, swimming around carried forth
by the strange fluid, a dozen or so little fish. the fish cavorted
around in a crazy death dance & when they swam off in the
direction of all excreta whirling out of the toilet the boy's eyes
rolled & he flopped down. kicked around a bit. & died. they
say it happens to you when you go poking your dick around
white places. they say there are other instances of asiatics &
armies of black ants that on going out of your penis give you
such an insanely sweet sensation filing out until the entire
army is out. & all the while you're standing around or lying
on your back taking it. when the last one was out though,
they followed the same track, but this time going back in.
they say the pain of it is worse than dipping your genitals in
fire. & they run tales off about other races & i've never gone
there but i feel an itch in my scrotum. afraid to scratch with
all those eyes watching i walk away. scared. & i swear there's
a smell of some creature or other inside me. it's getting out of
my pores.

but still i couldn't stop going into girls. but i can't kiss. not
when they stick their tongues down my throat. but it's sweet
when i'm between their legs & i go on forever until i get
bored or someone sees us. that's because nothing comes out
of my penis. my friends say it's because i'm still young. i've
no tjor. i could have the earth for a vagina & bring it down to
the tip of my penis & the stream would never run dry.

the street demanded it. they'd say about one: "ah that one
never even comes close to sniffing it let alone getting it...
the only time he even comes eye to eye with it is when his
mother gives his baby sister a bath.." & the street would roll
around in the mud of its spilt bath water sit up cackling &
wipe the saliva dripping from the corners of its mouth & see
how you were going to cleanse yourself of that one.

a girl eight years older than me introduced me to it when
i was four. i was scared but she laid me on top of her &

rubbed me against her vagina & it was such a great feeling
rushing up & down my thighs i didn't want to get off. she's
married to a doctor now i hear. but i'm in the icy tight grip
of delirium when i recall how my long limbed midget friend
who looked like a baboon... people called him bobby short &
sweet for bobbejaan but only when he was clear & away or
when friendship made it legit to, well his girlfriend was raped
by her uncle, a man from up the street. she waded through
the blood running out between her legs & came to him
clawing at the skin of the air holding on hard to her sanity.
& my friend bobby lost his. went to the man's house with
a gun. he said it was not the main article, he just wanted
to make sure the man wouldn't run away. he shot & uncle
paedophile dropped with a bullet in his thigh. & crawled
around the floor getting the place all bloodied howling prayers
all the time & invoking his mother in vain. bobby took a knife
to his fly & the pants dropped. revealing the monstrosity
the man carried under there. it was massive & an awesome
sight to behold. this drove bobby further up insanity street.
he slowly & carefully drew his butcher knife out & sharpened
it on the concrete floor. the noise grated against my nerves
but it drove the man's eyes straight to his groin. then it was
bobby proceeded to slice the man's phallus off. there was
blood there, & a wriggling monstrous sausage that the dog
next door ran away from when we threw it over the fence
hoping the mongrel would eat it. the next day it wasn't there.
hunger must have made the dog hang its principles. & fear of
the great-big-gravedigger-dick.

bobby was not the same after that. he went around
gunfighting from then on. & when he couldn't he played
russian roulette by himself in the shebeens. & the patrons
would applaud every time the hammer fell on an empty
chamber. i think because they thought it wouldn't hit an
empty one when it was turned around to face them. it
was until a bullet went through bobby's mouth & blood
dropped into his beer-glass & hit against the wall writing
his name that the applause stopped & within seconds my
boy was alone in a roomful of alcohol. & emptiness. the
self-preservation conscious audience had run out on the

performer. he told me he sat there for an uncertain time
thinking his brains would drop into his lap. when that didn't
happen, he shook his head a little hoping to hear the bullet
rattle inside his head. nothing. just his mouth filling up with
thick liquid. & a salt-intense coppery taste. he shook his
head some more & knew then the bullet wasn't lodged in his
cranium. his stomach heaved & his mouth was now filled
to bursting so he opened it & blood & vomit flowed onto the
table top. right in the middle of that mixture & surrounded
by a few broken teeth the bullet stared at him & winked. he
blinked once & winked & they were great friends. he walked
around for months with his mouth sewn up dovecote-style
with wire. he walked around with bullets in his body over
the years. from licensed guns & illegally owned ones. thugs
& policemen alike shoved missiles into his body. he came
hobbling around with swollen feet & legs once after he'd
jumped out of a third storey hospital toilet window where
he'd been under police guard after having tried to rob a
jewellery store & he'd been perforated by bullets courtesy
of the shopkeeper opposite & a policeman arriving some
time later when he was lying bleeding down on the ground.
sometime later a group of concerned law-abiding citizens
stoned him to death before burning his corpse for being a
nuisance that wouldn't die. the priest was vulgar when he
made noises about living by the sword. that sixteen year old
boy looked out for me.

i had another friend deaf & dumb. he wore a plastic bib
because he drooled buckets. you would be talking & laughing
& then have a spoonful of saliva in your mouth blown there
by the wind. when he ate, half his food went down the bib
& mixed with the drool & sat there watching you. but he
was a clever boy. he made lots of money begging while we
stood guard so no one would try to take it off him. every
time someone gave him money he'd laugh behind their back
& wink. & when the money was substantial we'd run off. at
times to the cinema. it stunk in there. there was a heavy
smell of piss that hit right up to the back of your head as you
sat there. us young ones would sit up front right on the stage
& the images would be all warped & wavery. lopsided heads

& horses with twin backs. & guns made of jelly. we'd go to the midnight shows. they showed people fucking sometimes if the features finished too early for the cinema to let us out into the streets. they filled space with those blue films. we'd battle to stop ourselves from laughing they'd belt us behind the neck & threaten to throw us out into the night & the cold so we learnt to be quiet. i was ten. halfway through the movie you'd hear groans from deep within the audience & know some were pumping & pulling very taut wires there. sometimes i'd see grown men with their flies open & their penises in their hands. the seats were wet often in that cinema. that's why they made us sit on the stage where the movie was so bad to watch. i saw people fucking right inside the movie house, they'd do it in the dark surreptitiously otherwise they'd get whipped & thrown out. it happened often because they were often too deep in it to mind the noise they were making. one man was thrown off the woman he was with, she was dragged off into the toilet & the traffic into that toilet was busy that night. i saw many men go in there. when i tried to go a slap on my face threw me across the place & i crashed against a chair it opened a gash in my head. the last time i went in there a man dragged me off behind the screen started running his hands up & down my little penis. he was salivating all the while. dropped his pants & dragged my head to his cock. he was choking me with his hands behind my head. he thrust it onto my lips. & darkness closed around my head. i was choking as i sunk my teeth on it. he screamed trying to beat me off. i was scared locking my teeth even tighter around his dick. heat surrounded my mouth as the vomit rose. but i wouldn't couldn't ease my teeth off. the blood spurted into my hair. he was screaming when my friends burst on the scene i heard. i wasn't aware of anything. i was out of it. they say they had to work my jaws loose. the man walked away with it holding on by a strand. my friends beat him up a bit & for luck they pissed on him. one wanted to cut the phallus off altogether but the rest samaritanned it. no-one knows if it went back to roots but it was dripping its life onto the carpet & the dust when it hung down.

anyway, my friend died with his intestines in a dish someone
gave to him to make sure they wouldn't drag in the dust.
"keep them in... if they catch any dust you're dead..."
that's what they'd said i was told. i wasn't there when a
man opened a pump action shotgun on him. they say he
chased his navel down the street because the volley took
him sideways. the man was shooting at another but got my
boy instead. & said to him to fuck off & die anyway for being
there in the first place. they spoke about it in the shebeens
laughing at the idea of my boy flipping that plastic bib aside
sending it flying in the wind trying first to get hold of his belly
button & then being swiped aside so my boy could hold his
intestines in. it turned from bright yellow to purple they said,
with the blood & the food & the saliva running.

like years later when i'm hanging on a fence & there's a
dozen or more dogs around my ankles dancing around
laughing. guffawing as the bricks come down on my head my
back my body. there's an axe buried in my skull & these dogs
want me dead. i'm wet blood dripping sticking the little fabric
of... ahhh. a knife slides into my side. there's a cut beneath
my left eye. they'd tried to poke my eye out so i couldn't see
them kill me. i've an axe wound gaping at the back of my
head & the wind howls trying to get into my skull. they're
gleeful around me. still the stones the bricks the rocks land
on my back hanging to dry on the fence there. some of them
are just children not twelve yet but that's street level reality. i
fall into darkness swallowing me up head first. i woke up in
hospital. policemen took me there in the back of van. i heard
that some of them were happy i was hurt & near death. they
called me jackal in the streets. but right now hysteria shakes
the walls of my senses down. forces pull my eyes to the
ground & i see my nerves writhing in the dust.

the leaders were now out of leper holes. the land freed. or
so declared by those who should know. the lot of those of
us declared undesirable ill-fitting mental-defectives were
force-fed a radicalisation. yes i woke out of it walking. i spun
out of madness when the land hurtled into it. i stood out of
it & looked in wonder. more, horror. society bared its fangs

& invited me between them. & i ran as from the nightmare
i'd just come out of. in the end truth & illusion shrunk to
between my striding legs as lights exploded in my senses
shrieking pulling at root-ends. the fear erupted out of her
eyes & pierced through my brains. she wriggled & it was a
rabbit trying to get free of carnivorous fangs dripping its life
juices into the dirt. it impaled me deep inside her being. the
sensation split me open. the idea of conquest sickens me.
as i braced myself to leap out i looked & her mouth was red
open emitting a soundless sigh. & the sun was coming up.
it filtered through to my subconscious. "it brings the reality
of things back to me." & she eased her hold on my skin &
bones. she'd told me she wanted me to come as i held back.
afraid to let my juices run. it would be even more beautiful
she'd said. easing herself open & onto my swollen cock. i
was feeling hot pain in my swollen veins standing navy-blue
against the darkness of my skin. then she'd started moving &
i felt my streams rush to run over. moments later i touched
the ceiling. & burst through as she pulled at my dreadlocks
& the liquid left my system to run out into the streets &
crash out through & beyond the staring windows of the
sullen buildings across. i felt an underground tremor the air
in vibrations the walls shook. i lay limp from the knockout
bout. she was smiling as the sun hit my eyes & went out.
through the ages i hear my mother's body hit the shuddering
wall & jar me back to now. the girl is gone so's the warmth
& i shudder in the heat. trembling post-orgasmic as my
genitals seek to disappear inside my bowels. terror & mouth
open surprise mingled. not so much merged as fused & it all
exploded in front of my mind in back of my brain. conscious
& subconscious met in the area most are scared to visit &
if they do, seldom come back from. & there i knew myself.
saw me & the world naked starklit raving gasping for the last
lifeline's brain at the sight of our own spectres. the mind was
skinned. its hide hung on the outside. in the blood was tears
dripping refusing to acknowledge themselves. hell blazed
heaven froze over & i was caught in the hinterland looking
in on myself howling "GO AWAY" to my shadow. it was this
place it is from this area of my psyche bared & starving
staring out that i bring myself to answer the questions i've

never before dared ask myself or any phantom else. what
follows is my testimony to the truth as never written never
spoken except perhaps in the icy stillness melting in frozen
hearts minds opened to heaven's ogre eye. unseeing uncaring
gouged out by bibled lies beneath conspiratorial pews. i don't
think it'll ever be told, being inarticulable.

the flaming cape fluttered in the blaspheming wind. IN
NOMINE PATRI... father mason hump-arched the small of his
back. the veins stood blue against the burnt-red of his face.
i saw the sweat trickle down his face from the bald path to
heaven between the bushes of his hair. i thought his fingers
were going to snap. the fence sang as he bobbed it up & the
woman on the other side pulled it up. it was a symphony.
his breath was rasping, hers escaped from between chapped
lips with the sound of pebbles rattling inside a tin. his upper
lip trembled as i saw her buttocks ripple against the fence.
they were glued to that wire. then she stopped moving & his
face contorted. she said something & he hit the fence hard
with his palm. frustration messing up the flow. i inched closer
as the woman gave a fast twist to her waist & the preacher
howled the heavens down.
"give me the money NOW" she cooed all honeyed discharge.
"oh blood of jesus..." he intoned.
"oh stop it up you little bleeding jesus."
"he who dwells in the shadow of the most high who abides
in the shadow of the almighty" without acknowledging the
recitation, his other hand fumbled searching deep in the
folds of his cape & coming out clutching some banknotes.
he seemed to be wanting to count out a number, hesitated
& pushed the lot through the fence. "my refuge & my
fortress" his midriff stormed her castle. she smiled. pulling
an inch forward, he gasped losing his line of thrust. both
metaphorically & otherwise. & got it back seconds later. that
great anointed man of the lord. "for he will deliver you from
the snare of the fowler... ah...& from the deadly pest...pest...
pestilence...shooo." they were still butt to crotch against each
other. she smiled thrusting the bundle under her t-shirt as he
got feverish. "he will cover you with his pinions and under his
wings you will find refuge..." he took a deep breath plunging

deep under her jutting butt. he skipped a few verses.
"you will only look with your eyes & see the recompense of
the wicked..."
"we need to get paid you know." she ventured, but he was
not to be led astray & unto the path of perdition. so, "no
evil shall befall you no scourge come near your tent." he
was deep & cosy inside hers. the skirt ballooning as a slight
breeze sought to cool that fire. he stood on tip-toe. her rear
end was high up balanced against the fence. he dug his
toecaps deep in the sand for leverage & went forth. "for he
will give his angels charge of you... to guard you in all your
ways. on their hands they will bear you uuuupppp!!!" he was
being borne up indeed. he breathed heavily, the veins lay
corded on his neck. i thought a pipe was bound to burst. &
the wastewater would flow. "lest you dash your dick against
the fence." she tried to help him out with the psalm when
he seemed to go loose of the lord's work. the sweat running
into the folds of the great blessed bloodshaming cape. he
switched to psalm 92, that song of the sabbath. it would
soon be time for a rest. "but thou has exalted my horn like of
the wild ox..." yes indeed, i thought, catching glimpses of it
as it slid in & out of her tent. "thou has poured over me fresh
oil..." that fluid was dripping between their legs & hanging
for a moment on the fence before dropping too indecently
unto the dust. then she moved her midriff from side to side &
the motion made the preacher peel his lips. i saw the jackal
dance across his features. he pulled back somewhat & thrust.
i was hypnotised watching from the corner of the church.
they made that fence sing i said. "...to the music of the lute
& the harp... to the melody of the lyre... for thou oh lord hast
made me glad by thy work... at the works of thy hands i sing
for joy..."
the sound of the piano playing within the church's bowels
made its heavenly sounds. then they started going at it faster.
the fence moved to & fro, father mason on the inside the
woman on the outside, with the fence between them fucking
through a hole.
"the floods have lifted up oh lord the floods have lifted up
their voice... the floods lift up their roaring... mightier than
the thunders of many waters... mighty mighty my my ha ha

oh lord all mighty mightier than the waves of the seaaaa..."
it crashed against the rock of that mass of buttocks. eased
back & smashed once again. at what seemed like the height
of that storm the woman suddenly jerked forward, sliding
him out & sprinted into the elephant grass on her side of the
fence & seconds later disappeared out of sight. the preacher
grabbed the fence like for his life, lips pulled far back teeth
glinting in the gathering gloom as his red phallus got into
a wild dance crashing against the fence this way & that as
fluid gushed out of it baptising the grass on the other side.
some of the semen hanging on to the fence, undecided on
when to take the plunge to hit earth. he screamed "from the
lord of hosts you will be punished hm hm with thunder &
earthquake & loud noise hm hm with whirlwind & tempest &
the FLAME hm hm of a consuming FIRE!!!" at this point he
shook his fist at the woman fast disappearing into the thick
grass shouting "AMEN" over the shoulder as the penis gave a
few last / lust kicks against the dying sun making discordant
music. then seemed to hang its arms in exhausted deadbeat
pugilist pose against those boxing ring wire-ropes. but it had
gone at it bare-knuckled. now it swayed. its head drooping
in shame. he looked down at it in frustration & i heard him
turn earthbound swear & curse & bring the heavens down
FUCKING SHIT BITCH I'LL GET YOUUUU your mother's
arseho... he cut it midstream turning around. i tried to sink
into the wall but he'd seen me. & the rage of the lord spewed
from between his wet lips.
"woe to the shepherds who destroy & scatter the sheep of
my pasture..." he paused. "says the lord." he added massive
lifted in the might of the almighty. & i was so small cringing
in my transgression. as he pulled up his trousers that had
throughout the drama been bundled in a sad heap around
his ankles. "for you have eyes & heart only for your gain..."
he intoned on the advance. i didn't want anything from him.
"behold, i will attend to you for your evildoing." he had a
most unholy look on his face & the thought of hades' blazes
lapping my soul's juices eating away at my heart brought
smoke out of my mouth. but i could not flee from that wrath
swooping down on me.

later, he called me the devil's own sick child as the strap
came down pulling flesh off where it ate into my skin. he
was exorcising the demons out of my foul system. i was
nebuchadnezzar with hair on my heart, he screamed. been
sent to render muddied the purity of his soul. & the strap got
caught in my hair. it burnt all hell when he yanked at it & i
fell on the cold floor trying to get away, grabbing at a pew. he
was chanting verses from the scriptures as he flayed my so
human & thus sinful flesh with that strap. "behold, the storm
of the lord! wrath has gone forth, a whirling tempest..." then
a halo formed around his head & i stared. "it will burst upon
the head of the wicked... the anger of the lord will not turn
back... until he has executed & accomplished the intents of
his mind..." i was staring at the angels dancing deep inside
that light. that was the last i saw that day. as i sunk into
the pit of unconsciousness. the last line filtered through the
mist forming before my eyes. " 'in the latter days you will
understand it clearly.' jeremiah 23 verse 19 to 20. the lord
bless your sleep my son..."

next sunday for the first time i refused to go to get dressed up
in jacket & tie to get carted away to church. i rolled around
screaming & kicking on the floor & my mother couldn't
understand. my soul indeed needed saving. the grace of our
lord...

it spreads itself out with such warmth across the decades.
& pierces through my head in an icepick. cracking through
the ice of my young years. & it penetrates right down to the
GIRLS ON THE RAMPAGE. the ones i knew to the bone.
it started out when she staggered into my place & flopped
down in her senses dragging across the floor. & there was
muddy brown liquid running down her legs. & dried grey.
& her eyes were reaching out piercing through my head to
crash against the wall behind me. later she told me: "you
know bavino those stupid little horny cowards thought they
were doing me down... but they didn't know they were
actually doing me a fucking favour. it's just a pity i couldn't
even feel them. not one. not once you know i knew they
were swimming around there trying to hit the bottom... but

man, they should have got bigger brothers to do it you know.
i mean what's the use of a fuck if it can't even make you
sweat. even if it comes to you six times in a row & switches
around again until it's a dozen & then on again same way…
& most of the time you don't even know if it's in there or
what the fucked up little shit is doing down there i mean they
might as well have been knocking against my thighs…" then
her friends came crashing in. filling up my mind. she grew
up to become a social worker. stationed at some prison. but
now she said: "oh man they didn't know how much i was
in a desert for… what… how long i don't even know man.
when the last of the last rounders finished fucking around in
there wasting my time & they were passing some beer around
standing around not knowing whether they were coming
or… ah whatever. they wanted to go & i called them back &
they were feeling like little big men i mean… well i suppose
half a sausage is… i don't know they can't have been any of
them older then eighteen & i said come on let's keep doing
it boys & they were shy man because they knew i'd defeated
them…"
she & her friends formed a gang. & the streets knew them
as sharks. they did things to men. those women. they were
girls really. quite a few guys walking around toting restless
phalluses fell under the bite. like a man would see a beautiful
girlie & try to turn his luck in & well & good & he wouldn't
believe his own luck & think his ancestors were with him.
he'd end up though locked up in a back-room being pulled
pumped pressed & ironed out with all the seed sucked out
of him & still have to go some way still. there were stories of
grown men screaming way into the night & past the daylight.
all the while the girls would be taking turns with him each
trying out some new technique on him or one not exactly
new but favoured. the man would plead for mercy scream
shout & crawl around & get laughed at when not being made
to eat clits & buttholes & get rubbed up around the mouth
of the vagina. all of them. there were numerous such cases.
there's a man down the street who used to draw respect from
out of the flesh of people with a knife-blade. well he gets no
such anymore since the sharks took chunks of his flesh off
him until he was a shrivelled up worm dragging himself down

the street crabwise. he can't walk straight after the dread
encounter. the sexperience unhinged his mind. cracked his
ego against the walls. & came down from the laughing room
to settle & spread out eternally on his face. i've heard fools
say they wished that would happen to them & they'd "show
those bitches what manpower means... think about all those
female touches working on your genitals & all that cunt &
they say they lick you up too hey... & they twist turn you up
& down run their tongues under your hood man if you're
not circumcised & pull your flesh blanket down onto their
tongues & twiddle around your knob squeeze you in & out...
well i'd be so deep i'd be out of every one of their mouths
at the same time man... you don't know me..."   well i don't
wish to.

how long can you keep an erection up without the blood
rushing to your head & spurting out? it springs into your eyes.
floods your senses. & then the vaginas keep coming chasing
after their mouths clutching in the queue right behind their
hands working you up while you scream your way down
again & then try to rise to meet another orifice grinning at you
advancing to wrap itself like so many wet choking tentacles &
still the belt doesn't break. & you pass out they wait for you.
it's said the patience of women knows no bounds. well you
learn that on your back begging. they spread out around you
& coax you back to consciousness & you emerge out of those
depths flailing around for a manhoodhold. but it's them who
hold your manhood. sometimes they shove things up your
arsehole candles carrots cucumber & then their fists & it goes
on still. they try everything more than once if possible. until
maybe boredom comes down with your limpness or you can't
conceivably be gotten up & limping. let alone running at any
throttle. then they turn you out into the street. no one goes
to the police with it. they get themselves laughed at silly in
the street all the way up & then down. like that over & over &
the street's mind stretches to far places. so too its mouth. so
the men who've been there keep their arses shut tight. if the
sphincter muscles allow. walking with silence but loud noise
in there & outside. where we live i've never heard anyone
boast about the experience if they've been through it. on

the man-victim side that is. the girls tell me things. a lot of
times. they say because i'm a poet after their own selves.

FILTH CITY SIGHTS & SOUNDS

the city is sick. stratified with moss fleshed walls of urine.
smelling of liquored nights of carnal knowledge. of vomiting
in the flesh of the ivy of rotten animated flesh & skins
crawling thick with pus engorged sores. mud encrusted. the
man was grinning pink dusk. clutching meth purple in a
plastic bottle. boiling blood burning toothless. swigging at it
looking yet unseeing at my shadowed passing. mucus eyes.
a veil on the grey buried deep down behind the pupils... eyes
of indeterminately long deferred sleep... white burning cold
somewhere inside those eyes. from under the surface the
pupils flaming through. flickers of light dancing across those
eyes. looking in the corner like a scraggly wigged woman
urinating into the floodwater drain. pink down between her
streaked with syphilitic-yellow. the smell of the street takes
hold where my chest sits. these days the stench of blood
disease poverty hangs around & inside me. it clutches at
my streams stripping away flesh getting down to where my
essence resides deeper than my senses.

the man dug a stick out of the flame of the brazier at his
feet. burning. smoke rising when he blew at it from between
corroded lips. he grinned. digging the flaming stick deep into
his grey-black leg. & out. into the flame where it sizzles with
the juice of his sores. & all around the length of his diseased
limb the second time around. he's trying to burn the rot away
i think. or pierce it so deep it passes the threshold. he dug
it in. out squirted little streams of watery fluid. they were
running in my direction. the leg was ripe with putrescence.
he grinned even more broadly doo-doo brown teeth barely
standing out against the navy blue of his lips. he dug the
stick inches deep like it was going to burst out the otherside
making the stream of disease flow. he was deriving immense
perverse pleasure. i could tell from the look on his face. pain
on its flagellation knees. winced digging in grinned digging
out & the air rushing in there. the air hung heavy around my
shoulders. but it was pushing me up. some kind of a sexual

urge as the bewigged woman shook her flanks to make the
last droplets of urine dribble out.

the dirt on the walls pushed hard against my temples as a
dull throbbing sensation crawled across. he was looking not
seeing me. or maybe he was looking too deep inside me. i'd
stopped & stared. thought i was going to grow cobwebs. felt
like scratching the hair deep inside my heart. he wiped the
pus off with a grimy palm. looked smiled & lapped away at
it with a dark green tongue. in the little spot he'd just wiped
clean a maggot wriggled. a vulgar looking thing. it shoved its
head out of his shin. & with surprising speed he grabbed &
pulled it out. it broke. he swore to the blue gods of meths.
calling satan down. it was twelve or so centimetres he
inspected it with some relish for a while. smiled at it. ran it
between his scarred fingers. he was vacant looking now. long
walks of life on his face. then he shoved it wriggling trying to
break away into his mouth. started chewing.

the smell of the street pushed me hard upwards from behind
up-front & under my soles & off my feet & walking away. the
street is peeling away. the walls are strips of flesh coming
off. drooping down unto dust. drooping eyes of cold fires
hang themselves on sights passing through. the dusk of
time suspended. pulled me away from the shrieks wafting
blues-filled from between the pores of the buildings on all
sides. from way up inside the top floors of the sagging blocks
of cadaverous flats the drains bubble blocked & brown
seaweed green slides. the stench of unwashed human walls
sweating in the cold at core heat of drugs & the aftertaste
of flesh meeting flesh. the foul windsmell of banknotes
changing moist hands. the atmospheric swirl of the heaven
inverted into emaciated bellies full of noxious gases. they
are carrying embryos with needles stuck in their heads.
blood fluid ammonia from days passed & past. from above
somewhere someone's cut up flesh bits & blood drops land
wet sticky on my face. i gasp looking up & some of it drops
into my mouth & i choke vomiting it out. but i can't. bits
of it slipped through when i gulped. not hastening outward
my pumping system running. brains splashed where axes

dug in for a robbery. cracked bone. cut the roof of my dry
& unmethylated mouth burning in these debauched streets.
watching the jackal of time creep up through the shadows
of life. & movement is severely curtailed. the wounds bleed
anew. night falls crippled on these streets. the waste of life
falls into the toilet blocked all across the city. one big smelly
toilet. i can't get words out of my mouth. the trap's snapped
shut on a yapping snout. eyes are swollen shut lips busted
teeth broken here scabies rules. a fistful of hate cracks
against bone. another long as daylight coming across the hills
of smog. burning plastic drops on exposed skin. the coins of
life's gamble spin fall raise their tails up to the sickly sun.

it's cold in these veins of disease. pulled up by your
fingernails you think you know suffering but children are born
to fall crawl into another putrid hole much like your own.
on the corner there's one stringy eyed dirty yellow looking
girl rolling in the vomit she'd just parted with. she coughed
rattling my senses. a piece of lung jumped into her mouth.
she searched around between furrowed teeth & pulled it
onto her hand. she threw it into the gutter. it was jackals'
sounds when another woman came staggering down bleeding
laughing liquid running down her legs into the dirty puddles
in the street. a man clears his throat spews the catarrh
onto my shoe. i walked & on to two dogs fucking against a
groaning fence. tattered clothed dust-laden children laughing
watching them. a man shuffling in an apron out of a shop
with a kettle in his hand pouring the boiling water out on the
moaning creatures. still they don't come apart & the man
kicks at them & they howl. glued against each other. the
children guffaw like they'd break the windows. start gathering
stones & bottles & all kinds of lust-dampening missiles. but
the dogs won't let go. one of the children rubbing her crotch
faster & faster as the dogs let out devil shrieks, a glue sniffing
one drooled onto the breast of a baby lying on a little patch
of brown grass whipped out his penis and started pumping at
it. & ejaculated onto the baby's mouth as the mother came
dragging herself along the pavement. she screamed drunk
saliva dribbling down her chest. she polishing her areola
with it smiled letting her breast droop fall onto her stomach.

"come do it in me please come..." shouting at the hollow
eyed urchin she lay down splayed herself wide showing torn
dirty wet panties. he kicked her on the mouth.

i walked on slowly into the oppressive night. into the mental
asylum & out? i don't know. no use moving swift if it's in the
wrong direction. obscene sounds chafe against my nerves.
all around shrill voices call for the exhumation of long dead
ideals. food for the god of desperation. is it creation? this
pitiless lunacy cess-pit. push the infant thought through the
incinerator. that's history. they call it the great equaliser. i
put the burning end of my cigarette in my mouth. the forceps
between the legs crush the foetal skull. the platos of the
world suck on their scrolls. of time's rotten cadaver. every
membrane in my body vibrates insane. a bolt of thought rolls
around in the mud of idiocy. defeated. give me hate i can't
be a dove. i came across human mince on special in the
butchery. & the masses shoved & jostled.

find now i'm dragging myself through my own vomit. i've my
own boot at the back of my head. drowning myself in filth.
living between the cross-hairs of a microscope the infra-red
traces my head. my detractors have erected electric chairs for
me. in my head. they charge explosives with globs of brain &
that's nakedness's violence extreme. across the music plays
satanwards & evangelists are hysterically unravelling the
devil set pattern. demon possession noises. this is a state of
morality & religious values. spontaneity holds centre stage but
only in the imagination. heavenly fire bombings punctuate
affairs at hourly basis to keep the masses in conscious check.
there go flapping tongues of flame. a rope of sweat twists
around in a cut to the throat.

one in tattered priestly robes rolls his dead in a casket into
the yawning lip of earth. but that's a drain-water pipe & the
rotten wooden box comes apart as it's forced through. i see
a body in there & a smell rises but there's no telling. there
are strong stenches inside me getting out at the turn of each
season. someone told me out here they collect blood in
buckets & the masses bring dead thirsts to queues. cut up

human meat is sold by the plate & that's a diet that's staple.
baby meat for the elite. a dying one is trying to drag his guts
into the gutter he's just crawled in. & the flies buzz making
background music to that action. but the music is slow. the
elements are enamel tonight. & it's rusty. a heavy mughead
conks an infant's skull but that sight & the squelch it goes
with is no longer sickening. another stuffs the mouth with
rags says to keep the worms within. then they break bread
with dead hands. drive a blade hard between the barely
thrashing legs. the body thrashes minutely. i vibrate on. still,
the doors of the sanatorium, the sanctuary against myself
closed against itself. i stood up from amid my own life's
rubble & am here attempting really learning to wake up &
walk. i realise i've long been.

i stagger my way down. dogs snarl so too children with
bleeding teeth & knowledgeable red eyes. on the hunt. fiery
eyes stare after me in this garbage dreamland. i've just tasted
beer's urinal smell. clean washed dreadlocks hung on to my
drip-dry skin. the chair is muddy under my buttocks. they
speak in an elusion of stenches. liquid. when he tried to
scream it was a gurgling drain-pipe in his throat. maggots
giggled & twisted around baring opening & shutting orifices
to the heaven of his brain. they licked their fingers wiping
the excreta off them in relishing slurps. yellow mouths oozing
halitosis they winked across the short distance of timespans.
when he opened his mouth to scream a monstrous hydra
shot out of his throat & liquid spun around while half of
it slid still into his rectum. blew bad breath in his face. it
clogged his nostrils dilated his pupils & in short sight whittled
away at his senses throwing them into the logfire of disbelief.
halloooo out there! otherside of insanity. it was a green maze.
walls of drooping eyes straining towards gravity. machines
roaring in the depths of torture… a naked being swung.
hung from ooze suspended form clay antennae… drowning
in rusty machinery's tentacles & snouts vomiting sulphuric
acid onto his head peeling slow minute by stringy mangled
flesh minute… fire & brimstone lord have mercy… it bubbled
in his stomach in yellow coming out of his nostrils in endless
mucus jets stuck to the bed. piled up rose to his chest.

fermented stinking boiled on the carpet. the carpet growing
fungoid squirming in there small worms growing gorgon
heads sharpened their teeth on his wails. tongues darted
out licking his shit off his opened stomach. grinding in the
head. hammers fell the machines started up in his cerebrum
pushed wheelbarrows through his eyeballs. the humid air
came down. stifling atmosphere. oceans there. drowning
his mouth full of the hydra grinning at him. they ate up his
brains. swung monkey fashion on his hair roots splashed
down the tears dribbled down his chin. they rose up. purple
lips licking at his groin. it was a tingling sensation shooting
up his penis' root. gorging on the scalloped head. he sat up.
a smile forming. that was when the sharp little piranha teeth
dug deep & flashed red liquid. wet. the semen splashed out
of his sliced testicles warm quickening to steam. stinking
vapour hung heavy on his nose. it burned heavy dropping
loads of crap on his mouth. the hydra ducked out of range.
his mind was almost gone & finished. still they dipped for a
last draw. a crab clenched a fist around his lung & he would
have coughed had his throat been open. it tore & swung
empty out into the sun.

he was smiling. he was me. coming out of coitus induced
sleep. i woke up out of there declared not insane not
undesirable in society's pass book. pass bearer on to human
relations. the face on the photograph didn't look like my
groin. or forlorn or absent where it sat on the chair changing
it onto its side. identity parade! hard farm labour! fit for work!
the paper screamed. burning. its cry warmed my mind. they
handed me some more horse-piss. castle. with no walls
tumbling down my throat. splashing dusty in my stomach. i
sat up as i saw a friend. i smiled he scowled coming over.
another one walked down crossed the street to the other side
when he saw me. bavino is still mad i recognised insanity
shouting from the other side of the fence in him scuttling
away. the gates swung closed & i wake up declared not
insane packing like a madman in a rush to get out of my
head. & now i sit here try to scrawl to posterity the times
we went through to bring it here. where now the land transits
/ trance-sits in the hour of the black reign's amnesia close

to god. righteousness at the land's head waving apathy's
moses rod of zero consciousness. living on a free-base. that
is graveyard level existence where tears cloud the reality
of the riots in the cemetery. they kick up dust in the veins
of history's perjury. cast scrutiny upon the plastic face of
political surgery. moving from butchery what sanctuary for
all the meat shuffling feet to the dead-pride beat of the silent
genocide on the commercial highway to paradise joy-ride.
television runs toiletry commercials alongside gory visuals
of homicide. but soap water & disinfectant what inefficacy
when you're putrid inside. handing anal retention to the
mental retard. rewards for suicide. pain & gain stand on
opposite sides of the road. both parallel to manhood getting
hard on the flip of a life-on-credit-card. resident on crises in
a bosnian-backyard of the mind. but then hide & seek crises
abroad. but body count the cost where you scratched in the
flesh at the polls & where you piled up your benediction
on the collection plate & mount the search beyond church
school & state. that's when you spot the blood-cash stains.
at the point where there's no gnash of mental teeth or rattle
of dentures. the noise you're hearing is your chains that you
shake to make the dungeon music of captive brains. flushing
the nation down the drains of its buppy harpy capital's puppy
pretensions. i envision crimson in a newspaper headline
running BLACK ADVANCEMENT / PROGRESSION creep
crawling sinking economic claws in my spine. cold. breaking
my mind-hold on the constitution's pages. hurling me out to
where extermination is an ocean. rages. i saw the beast of
power feed the cannibal need primal to the human animal.
saw the control freak clique press a MEMORY ERASE button.
so now the future is no face no place the present is a serpent
swallows it. chewing away at the soft bones of this child
of a savage heritage's foetus. now who's the devil with the
cat's bell? the story none will tell. now the vile & the docile
reconcile differences. check each imbecile smile of a closed
x-file. it gives good head transportation service to hell. & i
walk the underground of poverty's navel. across the dread-
line. the stench sits on my stomach when i'm mouth deep in
pus spilling from the skies of governance's diseased thighs.
but it comes once upon a death-rhyme & i, multiple times

upon a birth-rhythm. now, who sings the anthem & who the requiem?

the window trembled shivered & broke down crying. he wiped its tears told it not to be a baby & a rat ran up & down the alley trailing his intestines. dope on its snout in its tracks leaving paw-prints of dirty grey. it was peddling, they said, his bile. (dried & ground to fine yellow crystals red tinged around the fringes. to be heated over a slow fire. inhale the smoke. saliva dribbles out your mouth. catarrh screams up from your lungs cracks its way through the nose the eyes bleed the ears run the feeling is higher than dread. or lower depending on where you want to go.) it's a first choice among parliamentarians & people of power. more the mongering ones than the buyers. the claws of a flaming mouthed giant freak fly locked around both eyeballs & pulled. carrying a sickly green the balls swung in the breeze on black-red strings looked this way that way & choice to slide to solid earth & run into the gutter. as they rolled in the dust trying to get away to the blackness of that not great black hole. the cat (it belonged to his neighbour, that fucked up one eyed red-arse r-x junkie who screamed nights & stared days) sunk its teeth into something inside the slime of mucus-spread to retrieve them.

he kept his grandmother's ovaries preserved in a jug on the mantelpiece. his mother's last wishes never forget where you come from. so he'd slashed the beloved old woman up on her death-bed. the film of her eyes had cleared as he rummaged down there. she'd tried to raise her head. that messed up the operation somewhat. but he'd smashed the stupid wrinkled face up with a one-two perfected over a decade of street hustling. it was a mess to look at afterwards but no worse than the red & brown & shit stinking fluid that rushed from between her legs. he wasn't too long grabbing & pulling at the eggs & pulling them out. in prison they did something like that to get your money after you'd had your arse swallow it. but he'd thought the fucking witch's bags would be rotten surrounded by cobwebs after seventeen pregnancies. but it looked fine. especially now when he'd submerged it in his

mother's amniotic fluid she'd kept when he was born. she'd
kept singing that stupid song all the time. in case in fucking
case. well it was serving a practical purpose now. he knew
it would help in case he were to suddenly be near death.
just drink the stuff & chew away at the other stuff & he'd be
brand new. reborn like the christians say. but that rat worried
him. he blinked looking once more at the jug. it looked like
menses on the mantelpiece. there was the stupid snake again
breaking free of those vagina walls. out into the liquid air.
smart somersaulting in the air & going plonk into the jug.
jesus, it was eating the stupid ovaries. oh no. just then the
rat burst through the window coming in. the cat & the freak
neighbour in somewhat hot pursuit. he looked back & forth.
the snake was a python smirking winking coy an eye going
open & shut like some whore conning. downing the last of
the maroon. when it went for the eggs the neighbour lunged
the cat the rat he jumped forward & they met at the high-
noon of a collision course. it split his eyes open. the bed was
wet stinking of his urine & faeces.

sunset scours the sky. the wind howls again. cleaning the
eye of the sacred cross. where the horned beast defecates.
fornicates in its dream of blasphemy. masturbating itself
against the polished gloss of the christ statue over church
hillside. it comes dripping over the long wooden locks. it has
missed the passion opened mouth.
"in victory comrade, we burn in the voortrekkerhoogte
monument the faces of tyranny on banknotes. here's some
dope for the junkie hippie jan van riebeeck."
"deacon... don't please..." he's pinning a little boy under his
cudgel. pumping hard & fast. on the wall the crucifix shakes
falls in orgasmic fervour.
"i'll gut you... little rot face..." he's trying to split the child up.
from anus up. it's world war live in the lounge tonight.
"gather around everybody. we now introduce to you a real live
flesh & blood victim of apartheid... bah bah blacksheep for
your viewing pleasure..." the applause rings & rebounds on
the fallen wall of berlin.
"does it speak?" asks the matronly wrinkled old nun rubbing
her withered hand deep in the folds of her crotch. somewhere

else the skull inclined red lights flash all out! gangway. the
salt whipped, the sails creaked the smoke hung down. the
skull sagged. escape thwarted. the belches hung loose. cool
as an "alright there mate, captain grab lifeboats we're going
overboard." the slaveship has crashed against obduracy.

the child turned in the midwife's hand took a big bite of her
fleshy neck tore through the sweat dried into dirty salt &
got to vein. slashing through. shitting the distance between
vulva & cot dead. splashed in the red & faeces waded to
the shore of a window ledge. bursting free. the half-monkey
from africa navy blue against flaming vagina chewing through
melon shaped breast the mother thrashing around the doctor
dead. stenches in the etherous air of dismay. the skull's grip
came loose. it shattered hitting reality caved in squashed.
the worms cut through the stomach of the hydra & the spit
& amniotic fluid & green-yellow mixed with red splashed out.
sunk teeth in the throat of the maggot & the python drowned
in semen & the stench of discharge & mucus. all turmoil
unleashed. flying skullbricks. he smiled coming out of it.

the sobs stopped. the blood kept trailing out. once again
the hosepipe whip came down tearing flesh & the child
was no longer heaving, moving under her foot. when the
child stopped moving she smiled. for a moment content
with the state of her world. in a short while she was going
to be pensioned off into the cold of staring walls & a skull
grim house. she bends down to wipe the drops of blood on
her shoes. the pain of arthritis shoots through her bones.
"little ugly devil dogshit!" she put her hand under the little
head & felt the warmth & the stickiness under. she knew
her hand would come back dirtied with all fluid. she looked
far away. across time & space to where she was a little girl.
it was hostile distance. so she smashed the child's head
down hard on the cold concrete. he is always falling ill.
weak constitution & skin & bone. death is a thought forever
hovering around in the air vulture fashion. it's fixed very tight
& close to him. "have you ever been without a friend?" he
asks me. liquid eyes stared away from me. five years after
that first day of pre-school. he'd been dressed up. cute. four

years old. now he buried his face under the pillow. & i shook.
i don't know what with. it wasn't rage. i was not about to cry.
nor break anything. i just shook. pain deep behind my eyes.

when he came back from school that first day i had a smile
on my face greeting him. he'd look away. not weeping
no tears welling in those eyes. just emptiness. his white
schoolboy shirt was torn. strips of dried out red criss-crossed
the skinny back. strips of flesh hung down in little mouths
screaming red. now each month he's got some ailment or
other. weak chest headaches thin to the bone throwing up.
he stayed without any friend at that time. the child writhed
under the woman's boots. it struggled once more to get up.
then went limp. the woman smiled. far away look on her
face. then slowly, so slowly took her foot off the child's neck.
the classroom was silent. he's been throwing up. "i must
never catch anybody playing with this terrible vomiting child
do you hear me?" she said to the wide eyes of forty-odd first
day schoolchildren. YES MISTRESS! they chorused. & none
of them was. for the entire year. but then, "catch him!" she'd
thundered & the children rose after the child trying to get
away. so alone. it didn't try to fight when the biggest boy fell
on it. brought it down to its knees. cracking a knee-cap. the
pain rushed through & out of its body. until there was just
a dull throb at the back of the head. it seemed to be deep
so deep it might have been outside. clinging to the skull.
& the child screamed. the pipe came down again & again.
years later he told me the teacher called him mister vomit
& warned all the other children against him. he was lonely.
"if god loves us all why does he make some people healthy
& strong & others not?" i tried to tell him about disabled
children & others who were abandoned & look at life from
behind no shelter of love, no protection against weather
neglect hate the world... i felt impotent.

they serve soft porridge in class in the morning when you
are in pre-school. dieticians say a full breakfast in the
morning is more than necessary for young stomachs. in fact
for all, young & old. so the child had been fed before being
brought for the first time before a schoolteacher. dazed &

unknowing. the first the hardest in so many ways. the class
was already in session as its mother walked out of the yard
& the principal had it by the hand taking it to its first class.
the tears welled but wouldn't flow in case the other children
might laugh. when child & teacher's eyes locked the child
shuddered. a look, smile mixed with bile, danced across
the teacher's features. & then the soft porridge was served.
under the hammer of those eyes all the children set to eating.
the newcomer's full stomach refused to accept the addition.
EAT!!! rolled down from the heavens of teacher's height. &
the child tried. the spoon was heavy in those tiny hands the
tongue thick against choking. & then the food heaved out
from deep in its stomach. the teacher pulled out a length
of hosepipe from under her table. five years later the scars
remain. i massage his thin body & hug him to my chest. this
is my son. last night he woke up screaming. i hate you so
much the teacher tells him. years later. she sits behind her
desk for a long time staring at him & then calls him to her
& says in a low very low voice, go back to your desk. the
child is me. trying to stop her hating me trying to please to
be loved but the hosepipe comes down hard on my dreams
skinning me down to this reality. emotions bubble, boiling.
burst & splash themselves out at my feet. settling down at
ground level. i sigh, pick them up & heave them onto my
back. & walk. once again.

at times the flight of words leaves my reality in the dust.
governed by the lust at the heart of creation. death noises
sounds of life's reduction i'm wearing skin around the senses.
i'm filled with the company of emptiness. an image i'm
acting out my god's pretences. every vein throbs a firescream
pulsing with sensation so violent it strikes the brain silent. the
mind a missile in flight its strikepoint a moment of climax a
fleeting exaltation when the life at the other end blows out its
candle. like all the mind leaves my feet behind. intestines on
my boots are red shoelaces. on the battlefield i'm my fear's
slave. i'd make a kite of my heart if i could fly it. here where
idiocy advocated the senses' persecution. bring down the
mental institution & free the prisoners of opinion imprisoned
therein. remember artaud. let each pass judgement on the

validity of their own sanity. it's madness that rules the mass
of human societies. unsaveable souls that cannot be bought
taught are caught put in chains cages peddled on the market
of deviance. crime is no cause but consequence of society's
rottenness. justice is its faeces. now defence is an offence &
that's our judicial crisis. thrilled fulfilled by the superficialities
we're chilled by profundities. existence starts & terminates
on the surface. we lay plaster on the shell of the earth &
the innards writhe with wrath. our harmony is dissonance.
throughout history mediocrity wins. keeps creativity in
captivity. deepest thinkers are societal pariahs. lepers of
thought. "break out the champagne dead brain. set in motion
the putrefaction of inspiration. it's the absurd that are well
fed on the worms of the earth. i'm not talking of the alfred
jarry spawn..."

the invention of weapons of mass destruction came through
man's basic need to self-destruct. seeds of pogrom are sown
in peace season. notions of guilt & atonement are pure idiocy.
hence the zombie ways of the christian. the bible itself has it
inherent. religion & institutionalised education have geared to
indoctrination of human mutation's creation. inbred blood-lust
creatures the anti-violence machine. the storm of civilisation
coming from high up the bleach scale. the tide of a
so-called normal man's poisonous assimilation carries with it
the rain of our castration. male or female. hack off the dick
or cut off the clit? ah the need to kill off political pretension.
to be steeled against romanticised ideological assumption
/ consumption. it's the road of salvation that leads to
damnation. anomaly is an absolute necessity. nietzsche lay
down attestation. it's sickening only in its normality. that's to
moral / social freaks steeped in perversion. ablution for such
as these is engraved in our constitution. but who's moralising
with their skull cracked open under the might of the world's
saints riding axes to the head of the line. their gunfirelight
burns brighter in the night. courage is born in the rage of
fright. them that fight hardest are the ones most prone
to flight. they speak in thunder who feed on murder their
throats being blood-oiled. yet the worst blunder is to inch
close enough to get caught in the whiskers of the puffadder.

what? the artificial light of legislation without sociological
information is the present's blight. all of us subject to
incrimination it leads to extinction when crime is put on
justice's scale for calculation. seek false system of values'
destruction & all pathological liars will howl from high places
resist raise abjection based on the falseness of society's
pretensions. it's a celebration of belief's absence preachers
will say pulling a hot wire behind the pulpit.

there's a rapper on the stage spouting a lot: "one two
microphone check… clear the stage it's rage in rhyme on
the stage time ahm one ah two get off the tracks backtrack
stand back back here i go info to flow as i throw got on the
go in moscow pitched a tent in tashkent serpent of legend
underground amid mass diarrhoea in eritrea emerged in dry
explosion in nigeria & in algeria caused hysteria in the mortal
area. sat erect on death electric fence border south africa
mozambique clocked on time bomb tick iraq no rain for acid
stain iran coca cola with a smile child pose for time magazine
corpse picturesque falling bodies are thunder in rwanda
porter cart cash away mortar opened gash in bangladesh
– checks from cracks in trembling lips of commissars war's
commissioners in russia injected disease bloodstreams of asia
collar the dollar fell in angola at the head of lead struck dead
conked namibia bonked the nubia on the sands & a pile of
rands made the till ring where steel birds sing the death of
libya zambia built my barrier against poverty's malaria. swam
in red oil wells of arabia. channelled spiritual famine in amin
even obote plagued uganda. crimson swine in the sudan the
best is… shit won germ weapons on the immune system on
the implode in those coffers it's a finance overload… basic in
hand grenades on the genitals. between sights of a cannibal
gullet. a bullet in flight towards a self-reckoning. felt a colt
automatic on the buck. someone's one time child out of luck
in a metal fuck. feel the mauser maul & they'll rush off to
die. but some are so silly can't descend to death properly.
attention seeking last appearance as a clown need lots of
time & a long drawn out sigh MOTHER HURRY UP & DIE.
i stamp tacks on necks register your number in the death
chamber lick up the facts i flip the dice with ease a one a six

come two & five my kicks are live on the mix…"

the grooves on the record the dj scratches bleed. slave
messages hiss & cackle out on caprise drum & bass respond
in thunder. a pressure omniscient. rhythm tumbling down. in
time to pulsation of my thoughts. self-disgust sets in. nerves
arrowed towards sense's mutilation. streaks of lightning in our
glasses. "death is damnation. toil for salvation on an earth-
base…" he says. this self of mine sitting across sanity's way
from me. after putting me under the microscope in his mind.
where charlatans of the ruling order struck to impotence fall
to silence. he has dread intense vision. in the bass' embrace.
he is riding the flow of sound. "this beat is electric under my
heart's feet." he is bubbling to the rage of the music's surge.
"this is a celebration of the dynamic. there's nothing static
in the flipped tongue's magic." he holds forth as the rapper
goes toasting. spreading his words over that drum & bass
foundation. & the beer waterfalls crashing into my stomach. i
throw my sight out of the window & it's false dawn. "the sun
comes down & talent is ripped out of circulation, man, this
land celebrates brain-death. inspiration is fed scorn & power's
torment weighs it down. they are trying to stop the poet
writing about society's dirt. make him sweep the street. but
the pen in his hand sweeps across the land…" i think even
his thoughts are kwashiorkored to infanticide. "mediocrity
is whipped into high fashion." we are a generation mired in
stagnation. "former marchers have turned into shit launchers.
they throw it down from the towers of power in those
structures of fear sitting high on the brains of us gathered
down there. looking up for guidance." he is crying. but you
can't see it. like tom waits said about romeo's bleeding. "you
know, when you bounce exploration against mad genius
innovation it bounces back in subversion & the established
value systems can't take the explosion." a different version
of man as magician got us in cosmic motion to know that:
"put artistic expression in static reception's detention &
watch the tension rise DREAD (f)artwise … what the world
doesn't understand it will tread-pound into the ground. this
is a mental prison state it sits on the national psyche. they
lock the mind in conformity's capsule. thought is a graveyard.

a brain-stun-gun-fare. we need to wage intellectual guerilla
warfare. from page to stage sail through ignorance's airwaves
ducking thought control's missiles…"

he looks at me as the dawn in drag wriggles its buttocks
through the uneasy window. "these are symptoms of social
disease… we're a nation in disintegration… need to go from
conception in dark dank corners into explosive illumination
action." the boom bap sound crashes down on our heads.
lyrical vibrations hold the air. we've made the mystic
connection. the bass breathes deep within the constellation
of our thick silences. stars die. taut veined to rupture point.
the distended corpuscles of pregnant universes. individualised
accent placed on seized moments. the magic touch of the
bass in pulsation erases the great negation. "it's time to
cease our spiritual erosion." red rims his eyeballs. "is this
the height of your pain?" light squeezes through from back
there in the depths of his brain. "you need to test your
tongue for elasticity. got to rap kick in confrontation of the
whipcrack mentalities now your mind is on the slide under
the psychoscope…" in the pauses in the dub beat he tells
me "we spout liberation man we spew emancipation but life
is… strife is… you remember the kiddie game dirt-rhymes,
the kind gordimer would call doggerel when they bend they
make you lick if you bend they give you a kick? it's a tight
hole fuck. your orifice of course."
& the other going like "it's easy to repent when your god's
a serpent one bite & you see the light as your eyes cloud
over with the night… we could go on like sow the least reap
the most the soul's sold the host… you know, the blood of
the world is my toast… toxic waste. that's what the rest
will celebrate. it was some kind of free association. what's
the enterprise? give me a quotation… in the laboratory they
contrive to lobotomise on the why of the dance & the smile
when there's shit in the pants all the while…"
there's a knife eating away at his heart. he's bleeding
too much now. invisibly. there is a silence beneath the
boomstorm. the rhythm bounces in the aliment. the words
move. there is might there in that dread-attack. filling the
death empty space. his sockets look like they'll rip free of his

eyeballs. is it the other way round?
"our pace is dictated by the turbulence we will till pestilence.
watch the violence spill from terrored eyes. that maps the
errored ways of our broken cupsouls." we chew on the
jagged edges of turbulence from the stage the david slingshot
riffs crack the forehead. the tone cuts through the throat.
leaves a bloody taste on the palate. but cats never get their
dues bassman. might as well pack up & stumble your way
gravewards. "the capitalist face of change is real... what?
fiction! no that's been written before. but look around at
bums blowing in the wind. whipping poverty is the yardstick
by which we measure mortality. yes, existence is a serious
business." they've excavated my glands these days i have to
sweat for my tears. thought takes a knock. often. insanity.
there's no pity under the power-block. all around shouts ring
"wish for peace is disease... faeces of a society of sickness"
they say aimed at heads of a state of unconsciousness.
we gather the pieces of our windswept views & prepare
to trip our way out & onto the dark treacherous incline of
human relations. now that we've gassed up our blues. me
& my other self. trying to find a way through the maze, the
deathways of the land where murder waylays... got to break
through the wall of violence to the otherside. not lick or suck
off its arsenic but... the lights go out as i sit try to write real
upfront & scratch these lines in the dark but the worms are
on riot a storm in my cerebrum. the medulla can't put up a
fight. derailed it hurtles rolls down the spine comes to settle
on my tail. blows away it flows astray. i reach out to grab
hold of it of my friend but... nothing. the pen breaks in the
strain.

WOMAN & DOG. man's best fiend. the worst.
we hadn't been there for ten minutes & cold out there &
sitting in her bedroom when a huge dog came dragging its
thick fur & tongue across the room. dripping yellow at the
fangs & all hostility not even staring me down giving me
disdain from its peripheral vision. & she smiled liquid when
it snuggled up to her lap. & she ran her hand over its back &
then its head. when she ran a finger right across the middle
of its head it purred. its tongue slid wet out of its mouth. she

threw a look at me but i was deep in a book by celine i found
on the floor. but was looking out of the corner of my eye at
them. i'm allergic to dogs since a police alsatian hooked its
fangs into my thigh on a ganja riding campus day & teargas
& gunsmoke had jostled for smoke in my consciousness. but i
blink once & the bleeding & running & a baton slashing pain
pulsing up my back goes away. the dog's tongue was sliding
up her thing. on the outside & then changing position slightly
it worked its way inside. she cast a furtive glance at me but
i was deep on the journey to the end of the night. & the dog
lapped away at her sweat & started going for her juices. she
lightly slapped at it. & i thought i heard a soundless STOP
IT directed at the dog. but it would not stop. by this time it
was pushing that great tongue way up her skirt. & i felt the
perspiration pump up from down inside my head break out
on my back & the heat rises in my groin. i penetrate deep
into the story in my hands. the dog gets frantic licking away
& she tries to push it away. but it has gotten a sniff & will
not be turned away. i hear that cats are worse at this type
of thing. being more given to fish than dogs. she is getting
worried. & my eyes hurt from being pulled into that awkward
angle but i dare not turn them away as she starts hissing first
softly & then going harder at it & the situation is getting to
terminal point and i halt the journey without ceremony. the
night has turned & is now marching into me. so i throw the
book away & in the same anger (or is it hunger?) pumped to
explosion movement aim a kick hard at the dog's side & send
it sprawling with its underside to my sight & a gigantic pink
headed erection between its hindlegs. feel like retching but i
go out reeling away into the street.

he was driving a tow-truck & an angered community driving
a naked man with white paint from head to toe before them
waved him down wanted to use it but he tried to drive away
& through them bunched across the street so they grabbed
him dragged him out & drained out some of the gasoline in
the truck splashed it all over him set him alight & watched
his hair dance golden with a halo & a red setting sun on
the minedump next to the freeway leading to the city & his
home in the background for wanting to kill them like all of

his hate-filled race. they hauled out the chains from the
back & set them like bangles around the naked man's wrists.
he had raped a seven year old child they kept saying to all
curious ears gathered around to witness. the naked man
covered in white paint had a monstrous penis that made
his transgressions all the more revolting. "i mean look at
that thing on him sies man even i would not give him any
if he'd asked…" a particularly vocal trembling woman says.
the crowd howls down a young woman trying to speak in a
tone going against the crowd's mood. they tighten the chains
until the wrists start bleeding. like the rest of his body where
he's been whipped until the white of pain was striped red all
over. he's staring out to nowhere. making no sound neither
plea nor insult just the silence of deadstaring eyes. there's no
blink in those eyes either. a youth jumps behind the truck's
steering-wheel. as many of the crowd as can jump onto
the back on the roof hang out of the windows both on the
passenger's & driver's side. the grinning youth revs the truck
it farts grey exhaust belches & groans from deep in the belly.
there's a young woman sitting on his lap & a leg swinging
around his face from one of the ones hanging out of the
window on his side. then the truck moves forward & around
the human-pyre the ones who couldn't get on the truck stand
around laughing at the burning man white painted with red
stripes & the throng on & in the tow-truck gathering speed.
the man being towed starts running as the truck gathers
speed & the sweat pushed against & into mixing with the
paint & blood then stumbles trips & falls & goes dragging
rolling first from stomach to back & then back again. the
paint comes off as the flesh does. the skin goes scraping
across all the streets they traverse laughing at him. then the
bones start showing through & knees crack against potholes
& jutting rocks in the roads. they tow him all over the place.
say they will not stop until his penis vanishes. the man's
mouth hangs open to its widest wildest & tries going beyond
that. screams shouts howls for a stay of that execution
escape him. he leaves liquid & solid on those dust streets
tarred ones gravel & the buttocks are frayed flat & the elbows
are showing as he tries to rise up everytime the truck slows
for a turn but goes down again & the truck drives on round &

round the ghetto streets. i palpitate still. he's dead. what the
truck tows back to first square wouldn't pass for a skeleton
when it moans to a halt of whirling dust next to the flames
gone down now. cut to silence. he is thicker dust rising &
the atmosphere is polluted tonight. days later the street says
his crime had been committed only in the mind of the youth
who drove the truck because the youth had lost a contest for
the jolling attentions of some girl down the street. where the
fire had died down now to blackness jerking a bit still with
breathing embers & whispering-ash. the ashes' mates go
hunting in the jungle of the ghettostreets. so death bounces
from corner to corner of the ghetto seeking itself as a solution
to a non-life problem. it's news.

total power vests in the LEADER & he wields it alone. throws
the crumbs to lackeys with their tongues up his rectum.
deified to death he's ceased to be human. there are no
faults on the leader not a crack in the eyes of the world. the
LEADER has suffered the most in his time so the LEADER is
pure. isn't that what makes jesus what he is? that his blood
flowed & cleansed as it ran to high places. the LEADER's
pain lifted him high above the masses & onto the head of the
power-line. all sights zoom up there. kwashiorkored eyeballs
wade through the mist of hunger & stare. hard. at the
leader's full-bellied talk. hungered tongues hang out providing
a thick-furred carpet for the LEADER to tread right up their
heads. the LEADER is a dangerous place to be.

& THE LEADER IS A HARDCORE "G" goofed on television:
"we are really between devil & a hard place... in fact the ball
is in my court... no no in fact i agree with everything... things
just go on as usual... today what is happening today hmm
tell me... no no how can i enjoy it... for example just now
that is what i find difficult to what you call interpret... that
will in fact stoke the fires of what is going on..." the camera
pans to the LEADER adjusting his hearing aid pushing
spectacles from a wrinkled nose sighing as from beyond the
grave. the LEADER taking a sip of water from a glass borne
on a tray by a young woman/man whose hand the leader's
brushes against time after glasspicking up time & (s)he

giggles minutely naughtily each time while he continues the
monologue. in changed gear & down yet another different
lane: "in fact my biggest regret is that i did not choose
a career in music…" so do i mister leader. my deepest
sympathies indeed. but "right here i have a cd player i've
tapes in my car which i play but oh… i don't see how i could
survive this country otherwise my health is so bad…" i turn
away close my ears to the leader's voice grinding down from
the television set. he's got other aims.

THE FLEAMARKET CRAWLS THICK.
disaster junkies today stood drooling at para-medics trying
to separate bits of bodies glued together by a body-seeking
explosive. then fading to obscurity & even beyond the
subconscious at lust flaming up & out while a couple of
microskirted tarts self-starved fleshless in unworn crimson
coloured net-panties ghosted through the crowds of catcalls
& wolfwhistles. there were soundless claps of high-heels
in the square. redness waving at those crotches. in the
eyes & around the pubes. one fateless eyed man selling
wire aeroplanes to fantasy's far-off places. bearded pilots
of playthings waving rusted playthings wagging tails strung
from bamboo swaying from there to cross-pollinate with that
explosion of pubic hair showing through the flaming network
of panties. an emaciated slip of childthing trembles fingers
towards a hotdog & thick workedout steroidal arms clamp
around its neck. lift it head high & bring the little thing
sobbing crashing with its brittle bones breaking sickening in
sound on the ground. when it's rolled off a paving stone it
dropped on has cracked. this is the security the marketplace
adopts against theft. it's sadists that deal with hunger
appropriately here. of whatever form. the security guards have
a constant stream of women disappearing into the toilets with
them. these bodies bulging in all directions that are real men.
breaking bones old & young if these said bones shiver in the
direction of other people's property without authorisation.
off to the side a soundsystem beats against the human heat
pounding out a soundtrack of corroded jazz rhythms crackling
from throats of 1950s generation skokiaan & tap-dancing
oldtime men on makeshift stage worm eaten boxes of rotten

eggs. the sight tells me cockroaches finger the serrated edges
of the dirty bloodsmudged skirts short enough to not even
exist. goggles tremble in applause for the parade of cattle
flesh from the straining pants at the ringside. chicken sounds
emanate cackling clucking from inside holed drinkfilled barrel
chests. across the square an old white couple is packing
away their used unsold jim reeves serenading his god's
compact discs. these days believers want their church music
squealing hellfire manic. here's a queen classed on the tenth
count tucking her dresses between gargantuan wrinkled
thighs shiny blond with brilliantine / peroxide. pineapples
explode on wooden stalks in multi-colour. it's like skinned
human hanging feet-first. there's a bomb with a stubbled
lip. arsenic spiced. there are flowers dumped in rubbish bins
flashing red lights going off into the distant dark. here's this
human bag in the eyes of the gold-rimmed bespectacled
world slouching where itchy fingers dip into toothless mouths
rub purple gums to dig cooling alimentary canals burning
with methylated spirits. holding out burnt hands for sick alms
handed out with the pride of opulence. the market is overrun
with fleas. i'm dirty & love my filth. so.

fear falling free
on the eyes of the night
accentuates eternity in darkness.
glass eyes shatter
in detonations of explosive pupils.
kiss the sky's tongue in the slit
between parted clouds.
hair pierces through spills brains
lips of love spew venereal smiles.
& i bow before myself
blessed in my own knowledge.
this is where the focal point gets vocal.
air whispers in crimson crystal places.
in the cold wet depths of
fire.

corpse deep in the dead line. they take aim & FIRE. pulverise
the fire of their own ignorance. cold blasts. dry liquid in

desert throats. cordite writhes in ignited minds. murder as
catharsis. purgation they call it. devil. death of society for
the cleansing of mankind. putrefaction. cremation. cemetery
flowers. welcome to the cross. raise a hand to pillage. at
the rainbow's end is the age of the death band gore-lipped
image on life's front-cover. death is source of amusement in
the tabloids. blood laughter's crack of leaden humour. I'VE
LEARNT TO EAT CARRION. word. sit at table with the smell
of blood. walk death world streets. i heal my mental wounds
with my own decapitation. "the cut off head had sense at
burial… sent out greetings to posterity" a cannon wags a
tongue. civilization by brutal force. a sword shakes hands.
mutilation leaves a postcard smile where flesh met steel.
drops of red. rose. wine. the ancient smell of love symbols.
beauty. i've the paranoia of skin rotting. call the saints &
angels i catch demons in the wind. new visions fill the night
with human decay. in my hands. i mould the light crush it
out & smile at the gods of derangement. cretinous beings.
cold grins of mirthless steel. grey visions of iridescent skulls
"i'll make a catapult of your spine…"

dumb volcanoes yawn THE HOUR OF DIALOGUE. day
shattered heads of midnight. sprawled across distances of
blasted silences. broken slogans of snapped veins writhe
about in the dust. are kicked back to life. the next cause
demanding. the gutted air is ranked & filed under card-up
sleeves. rats jump out of heaven mouths. cyclops farts in the
mouth of history. from the first fires' lies to ones beyond the
tenth commandment. there lies the stench of hallucination.
alongside evil i see people. sun & moon sights & sounds.
the terror of my own rejection is the whirlwind whipping my
sights into place in the fraternal order of things. welcome. call
it cyclone spit bubble acid madness amid the dust & bleed.
steel hooks bullets bombs knives & the DAMOCLES spirit.
illusion & its denunciation. scatological views. the LEADER's
dedevilment wiping its snout / muzzle against the undigested-
human-meat-caked arsehole of mussolini. ballheaded.
the steel reflects words. negative. this bloodwordworld.
abstraction flexes synthetic on the surface of a homicidal fix.
complacency's dressed up vomit sprung to naked life. rolled

behind clotted wound mouths. & the body of my thought
sprawls bleeding in the dark / blind alley of impulse. acrid
VAPOUR OF DEAD BODIES SPREADS INTO RESTAURANTS.
dining houses. where future abortions wail. the grave's
excreta. washed in the false euphoric atmosphere's realms
of butchered dreams. nothing illuminates in the sun's black
convulsions. in connections to cosmic madnesses. harnesses
of broken winds. strangled between earthroots & comet-roofs.
i'm mutilated to immortality. caught in spirals of civilised
violence. burning in the hands of the kafka experience. under
the helmet of midnight, dusty memories are hanged to dry.

in THE TIME OF NO SPACE.
& utterances buried deeper than silence strike the head. &
the scream is a bell ringing tolling the time of hell come
down. i caught the discordant song in the wind & brought
it home to my mind. past the death of the sun beyond the
quiet otherside of shattered moonlight's tumult with dried
out spittle in the dust's jammed senses. mucus congestion
in harmony with chanted death slogans' movement with
slow menace of disease obscene voice-dances in darkness.
images so gone to waste they've turned prophylactic. put the
puerile flesh of deathstreet for a bandage around the northern
suburban bleeding heart. sway shift shuffle in rot of a prison
mental state & i mourn my derangement. where they ate their
shit & while it still hangs from decayed teeth, they gulp down
a sob & hit their palms swollen in applause for their own
sickness. break all their bones pushing the other crap spilling
from bloodstuck mouths. me, i've grown averse to death's
celebration as at heart molten tears from bubble crash out to
flood my situation. i crash landed head-first on this planet.
without a helmet. got splinters of bone deep in my brain.
making me see only pain. that was why he got me into a
mental institution.

THE LEADER.
the air is a wall of human swollen thick as hate. but here
also, THE LEADER's words reach & wring soft red-ingrained
fingers of manicured aroused senility. & the lip salve
declares "no sex for recreation we're all threatened with

extinction from now henceforth all sexual congress shall be for procreation purpose. & even then, only under extreme inspection." his speeches no longer end with the cry of POWER to the PEOPLE!

it's weak amid the mingled smells of rotting food rising from & to diseased bodies. it's a spectre of abandonment. the stench of death hangs heavy sways drunken across the land. body fluids are weapons of war. blood lurches across the road rolled into locked-up bolted & shuttered houses. even here electric currents are let loose on erogenous zones. & a moan flashes white wail accelerates past my jammed throat. catharsis' inferno beckons. from hesitation. then resolution. until advance there's terrible calm in my own denial. the itch is intolerable yet the scratch fatal. there's a rabid bark at every arc of my turn to peace. the dusky soothing caressing voices of the void promise warm embrace.
"sorry i'm broke sister..."
"yeah like the cock. cheap fuck. it's so broke you can't put it up on a stretcher..."
got to keep in forward motion ever doomed for descent into the honeyed maelstrom bloodied in season. & there are electric shocks in the firestorm when your heart is dipped deep in it. i plunge into the depths of agony my nerves bristle in flame teasing flesh the heartbeat explodes & is obliterated from under my feet. then "burn" shouted rusty though violent language oiled tongues that creak on rotten hinges. i try to run but their presence keeps me walking. deeper. into madness of my time & place. where somewhere the eyes of hysteria greet the breaking morning. the mourning has long ceased no one cries human anymore. silence holds every corner of this sight. whispers of dry throats drag themselves across the terrain of pain. there are stares across hostilities' near distances.

the years converge on my mind. & merge get fused bore through to the otherside. people events times all conspire to occupy my mental space. i can't make out when what happened. but all moments are transition time. so i move. everything i've touched has shaped me. left its mark in my

psychological make-up. but i'm so marked i can't scratch
over it run a rag over that dusty surface & see the original
being. "we love the guns when rigor mortis tenses..." sounds
crash against motorcars & people in the sweat of indifference
walking around in a daze. mix tears & fears & that's a stew to
serve to the world. all eyes rest on the land & it's red-tinged
gold on the horizon. death sustains this human creature. if no
other exists it will swallow its own head.

"we love the guns when the pistol-fly-wheel turns..." we live
in a degenerate place. but hell is a word we can't spell.
"we love the guns with all our thirteen senses..." someone
pushes the stop button but the activity captured therein
breaks through & the crimson is in no traffic light but
burning out of some one-time child. they eject the cassette
& it's another shell. another sings about the death-smell. &
still some more about the smell sight & sounds of a bottle
breaking deep inside a vagina. we've got slivers of glass
deep inside my brains. that's why blood rains out of those
that shout & yell thinking there's a story to tell about it. one
young & mandrax-bold one is trying to dip his head inside
a gun-clip. one soul sold long before it's grown old. but the
climax... where is it in this story book? the scrutiny is in the
wrong place.

a group shakes a man down & he does. trembles looking
intently down the barrel they threaten to shove up his
rectum. & as he shivers humanity passes by laughing at the
spectacle. it's become a joke as a shot opens an air-path in
his leg & the masses walking by guffaw rattling their dentures
when he screams out begging for forgiveness for walking on
the wrong side of this life's road. you define your life by how
you defend yourself. that is the street's philosophy. a few join
in the carrion-picking walk up & kick him where he lives. a
couple come by the man disentangles himself from the heat-
strong-hug jumps & lands right on the bullet wound on the
leg of the wretched one of & on the earth. with syrup in the
smile turns to the woman & she reciprocates & with fool's
logic asks: "what's he done?" he with his features stuck in
freeze-man-eating pose: "i don't know... he is isn't he... well

that's enough..." they walk by bouncing on love's soles. a
noise of the wild at killtime jerks at my senses.

the smell of human excreta calls you from across the street
before you see the one public toilet. urine & liquefied waste
matter & paper ranging from toilet tissue to bits of newspaper
& cardboard box flows out into the street. there's a serpentine
queue there turning around the corner. the head deep inside
the dark door. the tail shuffling about in patience's loss.
asking: "hey maaan why don't you fuckers finish in there we
have work to do some of us." each is awaiting fulfilment. a
hole to fill each man there. the same one. i'm told with an
expression of conspiracy when i ask somewhere around the
reptile's belly what's happening & curses & insults describing
my mother's genitalia greet my query from the back: "hey
fuck you there trying to sneak in front there we've all got
erections don't we? get your shit-arse-little-prick to the end of
the line..." the froth spills from that rabid mouth as it turns
venomously to the man i'm talking to: "& you there with that
little puppy, do you need his help hmm?... do you want him
to hold onto your tail or maybe jump in there with you at the
same time because you might get lost all by yourself heh?...
or maybe you should send him to get some poles for you to
keep you above the surface while you tread around in there
like you're wading in mud you little worm are you a man or
a turkey-neck?" but the grin with teeth sinking into my subconscious answers before i kick the wind: "there's a drunken
woman in there go to the back if you want your share...
better hurry... she might die before your turn comes..." dread
prophecy as he laughs out loud rippling the sewer-stream. &
then continues stirring the excreta with his tongue: "by the
time you get in it will be like old panties with the elastic band
gone slack... just look at this sewerage here can't you see
the semen of the men who went in there before? that bitch
must be full to the ears with it by now you better go look
for some rags to wipe her cunt with first..." & he cackles.
drink had made her mix up her sexes. she'd stumbled into
the men's toilet. & ha, the god of all predators had wooped
& woohed. the man shot kicked & bleeding in the street had
raised an objection when it was time for manhood to be the

thing rising. he'd tried to talk reason to walking hard-ons.
spewing things about something wrong with pouring semen
down a drunken & in no position to consent or not 'hole
in the walking (in this case staggering) earth' so he had
to be taught to get the educated talk out of his head. free
expression of such flaccid views is a crime punishable by...
well, whatever a group of bursting penises dictate. i look at
them. they are right in the middle of the normality road. as
i turn drag myself up that street the sound of anger pulls
hard at my shoes. from up front-line in the queue it rumbles.
a group walks out of the toilet fastening their trousers &
slapping another one around."you silly little shit you've done
it puny fuck now what are we going to do with these swollen
things hm tell us..." they kick him this way & that & he turns
tries to run stumbles trips falls & rolls about in the muck.
they shout down his protestations of innocence. "you killed
her you fucking screwed her neck choked the whore you did
your mother's wrinkled arsehole! now must we stick these
things in your arse or what? tell us!" he tells in bits & pieces
broken & falling into place how he tried but kept on slipping
out of her as soon as he got in. he says eyes wider than
any grave he'd tested it out with his knobkerrie shoving it
in there & moving it around. no man. even a donkey would
have had a big problem there. so he'd rolled her around
grabbed her behind the head to hold her steady because
all the filthy water in there was making her shift around too
much. he went up her from the rear but it was no help. & he
got seriously frustrated because he was ready to come right
out of his nostrils & this thing wouldn't hold still. & as he got
frantic so his grip tightened. the slime & broken down solids
got in her hair ran up her nose her mouth & then she wasn't
moving anymore. the moans stopped. & the other men's
passion ran & went up a different alley.

the stench descends to the bottom of my stomach. & i
lose balance & skid on the slippery ground of my senses. i
realise it's a tussle working on the olfactory. the stench i've
carried for years inside struggling against & perhaps hoping
to embrace the one from out here. where animal need-
maddened eyes hostility sharpened cut as they stare through

my nerves. i gather them up from the mud in the spit-rain
& sewerage spill & point my toes in the direction they were
before i stopped to feed my need for knowledge of my age.
ah, time comes stroking its beard aimed rope-like at my neck.
still another one staggers out of the toilet drooling rubbing his
crotch lips stretched around his head. but i'd heard she was
dead. still the look of lust whipped to satisfaction cannot be
captured on billboards.

time floods my mental space i said. years converge & it's
occupation time inside my head. my mind… it's all fractured.
fragments. bits. pieces. broken. i try to gather my thoughts.
but i can't hold them down enough to make sense. they pin
me to the ground i carry inside me. knead my brains in the
muddy waters of my existence. they take me over. fly my
imagination's rotten remains in the wind. broken at every
turn of my moments' parted buttocks. time talks to me. i
don't hear it. still, across zones & spaces lineage pulls at my
roots. my blood-tree shakes in the foul wind & rain attack.
got to dig myself in somewhere. find loam & spread. but i die
if i don't move. motion sustains me. when my grandmother
died she called out to her ancestors to pardon & protect
her son. when his brother her other only son died he was
cursing them. both the living & the dead. i taste the human
flesh & blood mash in the putrid wind. heavied. it starts to
rain. & the blood & rainwater mix & the mud is as it has
always been. like me. right down from beyond even my own
creation. brown. the colour of faeces. it lies with a stench
splashed all over my imagination.

like that life spilling out of the smashed windows of the
car that's just come down on its head screeching its death
around the corner. it turns over seeking some balance
bounces around a bit on its wheels then going down under
the call of gravity & putting its belly to the whatever little sick
sun & rain & mud clings to its sides. before the sounds die
down a group puts its hormones to rest when another call
is in the air. louder. more urgent. they run & my heart nods
its head at the sight of humanity shining through the gloom.
i drag my broken shoes that way & hit again an imaginary

wall. they've pushed through the broken windshield. another's brought a rock to smash another window & they jostle to get past the blood soaking the car & the injured chest behind the steering wheel. no the steering wheel is deep in that chest & there are spears of broken ribs looking me full in the face. sharp. eyes of hate.

the crowd pushes in to get at the victim's pockets. the said injured one inside the car's head lolls shakes a little from side to broken back side & i read the gesture as a vain whispered NO in the storm. these hands are indeed helping. that is, themselves. "well if we don't they will in the ambulance or even at the hospital the nurses & doctors too are known to steal rob pillage the estate of the sorry patients who find themselves in their care... ha that word care ha ha ya they do from the assistant up. or down. that is if you want to be moral about it..." i'm getting taught by them who know this longtime street. the one who had the first hands eager to be of assistance gets kicked deeper into the car & the glass from the window the other one's breaking takes a piece of flesh from his face as hands grab pick & run with the banknotes he's just grabbed out of that redsoaked dying pocket. as he turns to fight for his loot a flying glass fragment slices through his wrist & his & the victim's blood mix. predator & prey merged in one. the sanctity of all life lost in the dirtstreet. this is feeding on death time as the prophets promised us. i turn my eye around deep into my head & back past history as i turn walk away.

SMOKE IN GRANDMA'S HANDS.

there is a lot of smoke in the air. it strikes deep into my
nose & through my roof & the thought of GRANDMOTHER'S
HANDS shoves itself to the centre of my imagination's stage
when bill withers blows out ruffling the leaves inside my
head. grandmother's hands. my grandmother's were little
wrinkled light brown & when i held them it was like she had
razor-blades clutched in her palms. the skin of her palm
stood out sharp in places. nobody says it but when a gust
of memory clears the smoke a little i see my uncle her son
my mother's brother slicing with a drunken knife through the
heavy air & onto my mother's body & grandmother's hands
defying arthritis grabbing hold of the blade & when my uncle
steps on the broken bottles of that memory slipping & sliding
pulling hard back on the knife blood flies from grandmother's
hands. & they were cold. always so frozen. someone said
maybe that's why my mother stuck it out double-edged as
it was with her husband. whose hands... but no, right now
i've got grandmother's hands tearing the flesh off my mind
as she runs her palms across it. walking around on her small
slippers & the smell of age i think it was flowing out of her
to wrap you around that shawl that had holes in it & she
knew how to make toffee out of condensed milk at christmas.
but there was hardly ever any money for it in her house.
just smoke. when there were coals or paper & cardboard
boxes torn down to fit into that stove in the kitchen corner.
i remember fires. driving me out to seek clean air out in the
street. i've often woken up long distances away from home
without knowing how or why. just walking. there have been
times i've gotten up & walked out without any clothing on
& people have brought me back. to my grandmother & her
house of flames & smoke that was even in her eyes. they
have seen her flock come & go & come back again as the
wheel spun churning them in & out of the street. walking. my
uncle's the only one who has always stayed. & that's seen as
evidence of a son's love. when she died i didn't get a chance
to thank her. or curse her even. because i'm here. always
here which is a place i don't know.

in jail some prisoners will slice you open & search around

in your stomach amid all the matter in there for something
they think you might have shoved up your rectum. sometimes
they're right & you're dead. othertimes there's nothing in
there but your wasted intestines bladder kidneys maybe
with stones rattling around & a little obscene outgrowth of
appendicitis & you're no better or worse. just as dead. but
in this place i do it to myself. & search in more places. dig
around more corners. that's how i came on my mind huddled
in a dark dank moss-covered little place. it was cold in there.
the spiders don't dare go in there. the smell runs way down
below your nerves. & when my mind shook its head with
its eyes opened out staring beyond all madness i looked out
across the ocean of my age & saw my grandmother on the
other side. it was a waxen figure in that coffin when they
lined us up to look at her for the last time. i couldn't see her
grey eyes. they were always an overcast sky. storms raging in
there. she lay there with the folds of her lids of her death of
her... she lay there folded into herself. they call it peaceful.
maybe she was. in peace. i don't know. but she'd lived in
pieces. all held between the fingers of one of her children.
& when he opened his hands they scattered in the wind.
fragments of grandmother. put your hand out over your mouth
when you yawn. or cough. it might be tuberculosis you catch
in the air with your mouth gaped wide but i know i wouldn't
like you to swallow a bit of my grandmother. she was just
there. & not. all of her. & i wanted to see her hands. they
used to milk all the filth out of chicken intestines & it would
slide out. in liquid streams of brown. then she'd fry them.
with onion & tomato gravy on mieliepap it was fun time
meals at times. she was the roads she'd walked to bring us
here. from some path between rows of maize out in the fields
of her youth bent under the sun rain & cold hoeing planting
reaping a sack of mielie-meal some vegetables & that's more
or less it. the rest of it was the farmer's on whose land she
lived. in a mud hut full of dried cowdung fires. & smoke. she
raised my mother to be a machinist in a garment factory.
& i wanted to see her hands. she didn't die with her bones
crumbling under the rock of age... or any disease that goes
with it. at the funeral my uncle bawled out weeping the
hardest & the world comforted him. being the youngest. even

if he was old enough to have children strewn all over the
township. still he was her child & taking it the deepest which
must show his love. the only other son had died ages ago
fever-ridden frozen out in the cold on the stoep after they'd
had a falling out.

the two sons. filial interests clash to mortal levels at times.
he killed my dog too. hacked it with an axe because it was
making so much noise he couldn't sleep. its barking pierced
through the alcohol clouding his mind. he chopped it up.
that shaggy dog of mine i called holsum because it was so
white. it had fur long & thick & my mother had brought it
for me from somewhere i did not wait for her to finish telling
me. when its moans its deathcries hit against my chest from
inside & i cried he hit me against the wall. his fist cracking
on & beyond my ear. & it's a storm of pain in there. the wind
outside howls my memories down. but they will not lie there.
they get up on hands & knees. tremble in the fever of age.
struggle onto their haunches. & against all gravity rise up
& out of my fingers. that's where i clutched the axe. tight.
& sweat rolled down my face slipped down my neck slid
in oiled motion on the tracks of my spine & came to settle
with a tickle on my tail. & i looked at him lying there with
his mouth open showing yellow teeth & a cunt-pink cavern
where a fly peeped in, out, looked around & at me, wrote me
off & dipped in to emerge triumphant with a piece of rotten
meat pulled out from a crack between unwashed teeth & took
leisurely wing squirting me with some liquid excreta on its
way past. i raised my other hand & wiped the waste off my
brow as i debated whether to aim a blow at it instead. but
no. there are parasites & there are… well.

he had a different woman everytime. when he had no woman
with him we'd share the single coir mattress & i'd hate him
grabbing hold of me through his wet-dreams & pumping up
against my back & i'd try to put some distance between us
& fall off & onto the concrete floor. it was cold on that floor.
i'd get back under the thin blankets & he'd squirt gel on my
flesh & i'd hate getting up to go wipe it off get the stench
of that rot off my skin but i couldn't. never. i wrinkle my

nose under the smell's assault. but when he had a woman
with him, well, before the end of it he'd end up beating her
up, all of them got smashed out into the night. but anyway
when it was sleeptime & a woman was sprawled out opened
out to him, that's when i'd pull out the dirty clothing & torn
sacks out of the cardboard bin in the corner of grandmother's
bedroom & drag them in a heap down to the corner & lie
down on that mound. & there was a human smell to that
bedding. some of the clothing used to belong to my other
uncle. the one who died freezing just outside the door. & after
the heaving & the huffing, that is after i'd seen her do a crazy
jig pulling & tearing away in a fired up frenzy trying to get the
cotton panties that came down halfway to the knees off past
her welters of flesh... those panties – tough hard & thick, ah
the winter-warmers that they used to call 'oom piet' in the
street, or bloomers, guaranteed to stand up to any kind of
weather or body-fluid stain... they were often encrusted with
some discharge – after they'd come down & settled without
dignity on the concrete floor for the night, looking so like a
deflated car-tyre. after. & when the sound of so many gurgling
drainpipes going down & coming up out of the far corner as
my uncle & the woman he was with got fucking died down
i swear i could hear the sound of a tattered lung slither &
slice up my eardrums. & i knew my deceased uncle would
be telling me things. & i'd get scared & try to rise up to look
into the dirty clothes-pile that was my bedding & the woman
would say "the little boy is getting up" & my uncle would hurl
insults at me telling me to go to fucking sleep. but this day
one of the woman's sacklike long breasts was slung across
his face. obscuring his nose. the breast was all wrinkled
folding & unfolding in the force of his breathing under it. he
snored. the breasts rose. & fell. in time. with his chest.

images flashed through the years & were projected onto that
sight of him sleeping there. he used to be a different creature.
a man in love with a woman & çaring as much as that
situation called for. the woman was the talk of the streets. &
its flapping tongues & ears rushing to grab passing messages
in the all so kinetic wind. she was unfaithful. not once but
as a norm. he'd tumble home after work on a friday night as

the ghetto dictated & flop out on the bed & the woman would
check to see if he was conked full out & jump out of bed
& into the street. & the street is known for running women
way beyond the ground. & then it started hitting against the
corrugated iron walls shaking the windows down & cracking
through & into his head & he'd drink some more. when he
started talking to her about it, the street said, that's when
she saw how much he was lodged deeper than just her skin
so she went all out & into it full time. she no longer tried to
dig the matter into the earth. the street said she sprayed it on
her clit-head & rubbed it on his tongue when she made him
get down on his knees & lick it.

so one of those days he's brandy & coked out on the bed
when a knock on the door sends her checking to ascertain
things. then she opened the door & her brother-in-law, the
man married to her sister, with whom he'd been drinking,
comes in & gets into bed with her. but he got – i would say
wind of it but it was that much hotter & harder blowing into
his nose. it stank even more. it was more than tempestuous
& a bit of a volcanic eruption. they were going at it that
heavily. it sent him off the bed & cracking his head against
the concrete & then standing there watching. they give him
less than a look & got back to riding. sailing. boatriding.
horseriding. but he got out of the shack he'd erected in
his mother's backyard. when he was outside he turned.
locked the door. looked around for some wire. settled for the
clothesline cut it & tied it around the door-knob. through the
wall he could hear the sound of their groaning & grunting,
she was moaning like death was deep in her vagina. digging
around. he jumped the low fence into the house next door,
drained some petrol from the vehicle parked there into a
tin-can, jumped back & poured it all around the shack on
the walls the single window climbed onto the roof & spilled
all over. from within the sounds had changed & there was
shouting now. but it all sounded the same to him. jungle
noises. then he struck a match. & the place blazed. &
through the fire & as people gathered around they could see
the couple inside the shack mouths open in terror shrieking
shouting the horror of it out but the fire grew & the smoke

choked those screams. but still the cries bounced on that
wall of humanity. standing around staring tongues hanging
out drooling. the human animal feeds on mortality. there
were insane grins on those faces watching the ones inside the
shack burning.

they laughed as the couple tried to break the single window.
their hands got burnt & then cut on that broken glass. but
it was all blood running to a dead end. there was burglar
proofing on that window. to keep the madness within. not out
there applauding the coming of death on roaring feet of fire. it
was a long time before anyone thought of trying to put it out.
because the man who's my uncle was all wild animal tearing
around the area & none would venture to defy the rage that
was within that being. in any case, the people around saw
him in the right. so the couple burnt. & the crowd lapped the
juice when their brains bubbled. boiling. when the flames
went cold my uncle went the same way. passion-driven
crimes make the law skid to a halt. from the street to the
police station to the court & into the mental institution he
was judged insane. & he went with it. his friends the best
lawyers in the land who only never made it to primary school
had advised him to. & it worked. he checked himself out of
the madhouse & walked. back here. & was normal as the
next working man. that's the start of it. the women queued to
get fucked & beaten up & out wailing into the howling night.

& now here he was. & i was aware of myself & the weight
in my hands. i was watching him so much i didn't see the
woman watching me. i heaved the axe. the air was heavy.
then her scream sliced through it & it came crashing down
on my head. in the same instant she pulled her breast off his
nose his eyes opened & at the same time he raised his arms
& i swung. i saw bone show through his elbow as the crack
came & hot fluid spurted into my eyes. the axe was heavier
coming out than going in. buried in his arm. i swung again
& left it where it fell. deep in his chest. as i ran to the door
their screams rushed past me & knocked against the wooden
door. that's why it was so weighty when i pulled it open
& the wind rushed in blasting me awake... in the street.

going away from my grandmother's hands. i went out into
the street flashing its butcher-knife panga sword tomahawk
blades. mine had blood on it. up to the handle. the blood
was in my eyes too. splashed all over my mind. they dredged
the splinters of bone out of his chest. right there where his
rot resided. sutured the burst flesh & then they pasted his
elbow together again & he survived. grandmother's hands did
not. she slipped off haemorrhaging internally. blood dropping
on her soul. her son my uncle had kicked her to death. every
day. but she wouldn't tell. it's the neighbours that said it. &
that they'd peep through the windows & see him strip her
naked to prove she had no money hidden anywhere on her
person. nothing is sacred. especially when everyone else has
moved on. or backwards. that there was no way they could
have helped her. she refused it. it started with a slap & then
a teardriven apology. & it was like a mistake. & he got down
kneeling & wept raising puddles around his knees sobbing
out his penance & he was her son. so there were no words to
say when it moved beyond. he was not working & the woman
had stopped coming around. she denied any beatings. it
was her son who did it you see. it was her duty to support
him. having brought him into the world. & if he couldn't do
it for himself then who else was there to turn to but his own
mother. & i wish i could be a mother so i could feel what
throbbed in the uterus when your child kicks it.

when i shook the ganja smoke out of my head & looked
around i was at the bush college in the north. i can't tell how
i got there except to say THE MAN, meaning my mother's
husband was later to say: "poet... what is a poet? i put four
years of my life into making this man something exemplary...
& what does he do he goes & calls himself a poet... i can't
believe it! i ran against policemen. i spent some of my
precious, i mean very treasured, yes i wasted some of my
very important time in prison to make sure this man would
keep me out of it. & now what, hmm? tell me... he writes
things & then goes & makes some noise on some silly shit
stage. & he can't even do it well, mind you. if he sang
it would be something but what does he do? he talks.
that's what he does. now how do you like that... poet...

pooo... sies!"

all true. & he gave me some marijuana to sell too. so that
i could contribute to my own civilisation he said. & have
something to rattle in my pockets. but i ended up smoking
more than i sold & so he gave up on that one. & settled
down to some serious peddling all by his lonesome self.
with a little help from my mother & twelve year old sister.
& like THE MAN said: "this man's mother... yes... now
that's a woman. very clever too. you don't find that with
these beautiful women. jeslaaik! now that one... heh... i
mean i would wait at the other end of the line & get her to
take the child... this man's sister, on the train across some
four hundred kilometres with the stuff & deliver it to me...
woman & child. now that's smart hey? who suspected them?
nobody. i remember once they got to the station platform &
there were policemen all over that silly platform & this man's
mother... ha... sharp more than a razor that woman she did
not turn around or jump about like she had to take a piss no,
she went up to the police guy nearest to her & asked him to
help her get on that train what with having a child & bags &
things & the fucking old fool seeing a beautiful woman ran
around getting her bags & tripped all over himself thinking
he'd get himself an address or something & shoo, you know
how dagga has a way of stinking up a bag even if you've
wrapped it up in loads of newspaper & everything... but
anyway, they beat that one like they won a whole number of
others... when they got to the other side i'd take it from them
& send them back. i had rented a house there. & sold from it.
employed some three or so sharp boys & they would look out
day & night but still you know... these things happen & a few
times i could see stupid policemen sitting on my tail all the
time... & this thing here calling himself a man & a poet at the
same time... jesus christ!"

what it did was get me to meet people who brought some
sun into my life. she was a fun-kid with disappointment
written across her features who said of lovemaking attempt
turned lie-down comedy: "all senses awake & pulsing. the
clouds gathered. amassed. it thundered. in no time it was
overcast. foul weather up ahead. the earth was sperm-

expectant. throbbing. opened up & waiting. upon a storm.
the declenching of things powerful. there was a roaring
down below the nerve-ends rendering the ears pregnant. it
was bound to be solid. strength. power unleashed. lava to
bubble boil burst forth & splash & spill upon hungry soils
ready to suck from here to life... but when time came for the
fury... it was just... a puny sad faced drizzle from up there..."
we were lightning struck rock cracked up. & she moved
into tizzah's life. he was my boy. tizzah. the crazy guy was
zonked out of his skull. standing at the second floor window
waving his bandaged dick out to the world. screaming down
to the women walking the street with me with a grin: "yeii
shooby doobies... how do you like to suck... or do you want
to lick ha ha this ice-cream?" he'd just gotten through a
circumcision session at the hospital. that's the extent of the
initiation these days. i've seen & heard news of rural based
youth who are still taken up to the mountain & when they
come down they drip pus from rusted razor cut penises. &
it's said the elders who run these schools changing boys into
men at times are so perverted they make the youths eat their
own foreskins come mealtime. but my boy waves his cock
out of the window & that's his statement for the day & the
women in our midst giggle away & that's the way of things...

this one was called sigantsontso, the hulk. & he was huge.
a heavyweight as thick in the head as he was in body. in
addition to being a major ism-spouter. & weighing in at
fifty-five kilograms i suppose i must have been pushed by
feelings of inadequacy. but i slammed into him & the wind
came rushing out of that bag & he slumped to the ground. &
i wanted to fill him up with urine but my boys grabbed hold
of me & dragged me away while he was a giant maggot
writhing around in his own vomit. he's tried to show off
to the females & chosen the skinniest one of us to bounce
around. but it was mere misjudgement when we squared up
in the cafeteria on a sozzled up friday night & the place was
full. i went under the hook he directed to my head. the best
thing about not being heavy is that you can make yourself
float but just stay out of full-blown punch way & you'll be
fine. when he tried a jab & a smashing uppercut i went

under it again & came out with fifty-five kilograms of bone
to his chin & he sagged. i kicked him full in the stomach &
he threw up as the walls burst out laughing. i swayed on
my drunken feet as the woman wrapped herself around my
senses & i was king for the night. i went out into it later on.
& rounding a corner all i saw was a flash of metal & liquid
heat spurted out of my face. the nocturnal animal that was
sigantsontso had lain in wait where he knew i'd have to walk
across to get to my lair & had made the blade sing. i saw
the bulkish thing slink away. i was sitting there wailing into
the night when tizzah came up. my upper lip was split right
down the middle & i must have looked rabbity. when i got
to the mirror the meat was hanging loose on both side of
my chin & the teeth showed through however hard i tried to
keep my mouth closed & i erupted. weeping. tizzah thought
it funny that i kept crying "the girls won't look at me ever
again broer waaahhh wooohh…" forwarding that as the only
reason for my tearfulness & breaking things up in my room so
unpleasant was that fate. the more i kept creeping up to the
mirror to get another look the more defined the hemispheres
were on my upper lip.

i went to hospital & back & went knocking on HULK's door
before the birds got chirping in the early morning. they
had all their doors locked tight & were huddling inside
there playing with themselves i was thinking. the smell of
anaesthesia clung heavily to my nose making me nauseous
in the dead dawn breeze but i shook my dome to clear it &
focus on the task of rendering that ugly visage redundant. it
was still gloomy when HULK from the other side of the door
asked who it was. i pride myself in disguises of all forms,
especially the voice. i mimicked a damsel in utter hormonal
distress & the door-handle trembled feverish as he threw
the door almost off its hinges & exclaimed i'd bet shitting
a little liquid when he saw first the axe then my plastered
face immediately after. that door was still rocking open
trying to regain balance like his head. coming apart when
the axe met it. moving. it ran crimson under the lightbulb.
the big boy screamed & the walls vibrated. he was trying
to squash himself flat & i thought snake when he tried to

slither under the bed. the next dive of the axe broke his
shoulder-blade. blade to blade & the more solid come upper-
hands. the blood was walking out of the door. & he shrunk
into his own stomach seeing himself draining away. wide
open to the heaven that was me standing over him with his
life-fluid dribbling down the axe in my hand. standing with
the power of life & death between my fingers. watching him
plead silently. i wanted it vocalised. "call me god shit-head
fuck face cunt-mouth say i'm your god now..." & he did.
whimpering little puppy tongue out licking away. i kicked him
in the balls & went out.

he changed ideologies. & became a friend. & we went
around fucking up the ism-spouters. they talked the wrong
philosophies. always masters of rhetoric. they spoke in
quotations. & got all the girl-attention. that made us mad
me & my comrades. with & without our poetry. they could
move the crowds. & that was a problem because getting the
masses back on track after those mothers had gone wrecking
the shop we'd spent so much time setting up was an epic.
so the best thing to do was turn them around & go up their
arses with an electric razor. in a manner of speaking. but
not always. at some point word came down the airwaves to
say from high up the movement outside had declared these
people a major irritation. so it was licence time. it had been
spoken. by the LEADER. ours was to do them. & we did. one
jumped out of a third floor window & broke his legs when
we went visiting. when we got down there he was already
begging & had forgotten how religion was a sense-deadener.
calling upon his pussy-arsed god for services. that great big
fellow was snoring fast asleep making the clouds dance.
grudgingly, we smashed up his knees. some of us were all for
shooting him behind the kneecaps like it was said the i.r.a.
did, but the rest thought that a dead idea because that would
get the whole campus up. but that's what we wanted wasn't
it. so the rest of them would know in record time that the
shit was spinning around splashing on all the walls. but still
we killed the thought even more dead when we got a smell of
excrement & saw it was making his trousers hang low. we left
him low on the ground. the next one ran & turned around the

corner & by the time we got there he'd disappeared. but the
next corner or door he could have run into was nowhere close
to sight & we thought him a great magician.

sigantsontso, the great hulk, exhausted big boy, went &
parked his arse on a rubbish-bin across the street. he hadn't
settled his big butt on it for a comfortable two minutes when
the inanimate thing went berserk. came alive. witchcraft
material it bubbled up under him. haunted it went bouncing
jumping up & down under him like a leaden thing in
palpitations. or struggling against suffocation. sigantsontso
jumped up like his backside was afire & the bin fell & rolled
& out spilled our filthy man. another one down in the dirt.
someone was killed in full sight of a 40 000 strong crowd
in the stadium but when police time came not one witness
could be found to testify. & that's how my people relate to the
law. SIKHOSANA had come running up to me & MESSINA
where we'd sat watching not the athletics on the track down
below but the flesh fleeting about & sipping from pint-bottles
of beer in our hands. then the pseudo-tranquillity was slashed
through with knives bottles & bricks when sikhosana bleeding
from the head crushed out on my lap & raising groggy eyes
out to the weapons advancing i let sikhosana slide down to
the ground & stood up. there was a dozen of them. MESSINA
pulled out a panga & the sun shone on it going down in the
afternoon & the weaponry came forward. my what's wrong
outies met metal not flashing any smiles or playing games
riding the scent of blood & i knew it of no use being polite
to carnivores so i pulled the butcher-knife from under my
jacket. it was still asleep in its satchel but the army of twelve
surrounding us while the rest of humanity abandoned us to
the dogs wanted it awake. so i knocked it on the head &
it reared itself to full consciousness. i saw the one axe rise
to my head with a glinting grin & sunk down & resurfaced
slashing out & catching the man-boy on his chest. i didn't
think it had gone deep. but the rest came up & i forgot the
one & rode the skull of the next & the fluid ran out of it &
sprayed my jacket. ran down my hand. behind me i heard
MESSINA crack bone where the first one had tried an attack
when i wasn't looking. the rest of humanity had awoken

to the fact of their courage & had crawled back to stand &
cheer & the whistles flew all around my ears as i went forth
to do battle. five stabs to five metal flashing bodies later &
they were away & running as some of the people got tired
of standing by the sidelines & got chasing. on the radio that
night a death in the stadium was reported. i was iced. my
chest constricted. it was freezing inside. as i said before
nobody stepped forward & the judge let us walk out of the
doors. i still cannot understand it. but it talks to me in the
night's endless depths. in the next week SIKHOSANA was
said to have jumped exile's fence & gone to join in the fight
against the enemy within. after two or so years & when i was
a member of society again i heard that he'd come back into
the country & was walking around shooting people. one of
those that got enemies mixed up & thought the best friend
was one deep in the dust. i met him years later when walking
down the street. a gun shoved its snout in my face & looking
around it i struggled for a minute to recognise the face that
claimed i had led it to become an enemy of the people. he'd
been chasing after me for a while since he'd been back. a
rock at the back of the head from someone who lived down
the street from me sent him flying & the gun loose from his
hand & we sat him down close to dirt & spoke to him. he
blamed me for it all. it was me who got him ensnared with
my fool arse ideas & stupid poetry. & look at what he ended
up becoming. what i became was tied to my beginnings. i'd
just finished my last exam-paper & was waiting on my friend
TIZZAH, to write his last in a week's time so he, his pregnant
girlfriend & myself could see about getting home. that was
when they put him in the boot of a car stolen from an –ism.
his & my comrades. because he was in love & a baby was on
the way so he neglected his comradely duties as a result. he
had stab & hack wounds all over him.

how it came about was this young guy, younger than the two
of us whom tizzah had helped out in all imaginable ways.
from the financial front off his dagga sales to the life-loss
frontier. he'd saved him on occasions without number when
the –isms almost had him for food & tizzah had jumped in
there & a few of them had hobbled away their tongues deep

in their wounds threatening all sorts of comebacks which
never happened. on this diseased day the boy came around
to tizzah's looking for a knife because he was expecting an
attack later on. tizzah would never part with that knife of
his but thought he'd give it over to the boy, run across the
way to my place & get another one from me & see if we
couldn't go hold vigil with the boy. in the hope the –isms
would come around. we would have both wanted them to.
so, despite himself he handed his knife to the boy. asked
him to wait while he got his jacket. upon turning away from
the clothing cabinet / lockery he met the knife on the ascent.
taking him in the chest. it was too late for reflexes to be of
any aid but when the shock of it registered & he went over
that barrier, he blocked the second thrust & broke the boy's
wrist sending the knife clattering away as he wrapped his
fingers around the boy's throat. all the while smashing the
boy's head against the concrete. then it was the boy howled
& the boy crashed inside as the others, who'd obviously
been waiting outside for the signal, came in knives & axes
drawn & slashing away. the wounds in his body couldn't be
counted when they dragged him outside. put him into the
car-boot & drove out with him to some woods just outside
the campus. & these were our comrades who told me how
he was still alive. they couldn't believe they said. after they
stopped the car deep in the woods & set it alight they could
hear him knocking against the boot from the inside where he
must have known what the future held as the life ebbed out
of him. they had to put some distance between themselves &
the car so that when it exploded they wouldn't go down with
it. they wouldn't go where he went.

they tell me all this while they have me seated between two
of them in the back seat of a car driving from the cafeteria,
where i was getting drunk while i thought tizzah was getting
his work into his memory so they could be held tight in there.
& they say it like it's a warning to me. red lights flashing in
those voices those eyes. my residence is just up-front. i brace
myself. inching right to the edge of the seat. they think that
the serrating effect of the story. how it gives me constipation
the way i clutch my stomach. why i wriggle around. which

is where they are wrong. i'm setting myself at an angle i can better manoeuvre in. & getting things in place. there are two more of them in the front seat. as the car slides to a halt i lean out tap the driver on the shoulder, the two behind me lean back, taking things easy. they are cool guys. so cool they are almost frozen. the driver turns his head to look at me & i run the knife across his eyebrows so that he's got a curtain over his eyes. as he clutches at his face i turn around to give some undivided attention to my co-passengers. when they stopped trying to reach for the door-handles i sat around for a minute. & then the tears came. rolled down to my feet & got me walking. once again. out of another home.

(please put your forelegs together for the THE LEADER IN FULL EFFECT)
madame first lady dry pus speaks stroking the leader's slit:
"selective stabilisation is the only key to the vault. poverty is an exhaustive exercise my darling leader."
present wet nose: "hrmph"
madame first lady dry pus: "it's some kind of cunnilingus as
                        sacrifice. grovelling in the pit.
                        venereal demons laughing...
                        it's the depth of self-flagellation
                        looking over the stuck shoulder
                        at the whip-tongues."
leader: "hrmphh"
madame: "like a gothic temptation of passion fires in the
         castle darning stockings as sexual activity.
         spectacles of fingers fiddling twiddling scared to go
         between the groinal wrinkles raised the latch...
         finger in the purse"
leader: "hmmrphhh"
madame: "a mongol epidemic of days of locusts in the brain
         while the flesh burns bare as inflated spirits
         pricked of sense of self-importance."
leader: "hrmphhhh..."
(a call rouses the leader at nightcap. hitches the first lady's corset.)
brain-dead voice: "someone has pissed in the reservoir..."
leader: "hrmp...shit"

(the leader's fart cuts the line)
leader wet nose and first lady dry pus enter bereft. come
lubricant centre stage. wriggling worms. child flower audience
anticipating misery mime; wave petal hands in the heat of
the torment. fast blooming to wrinklehood. coming off stage
eerie remote a metronome ticking the dotage. the couple in
nostalgia playing a childhood game.
madame first lady dry pus:

       "the spirit is rich as a witch's human skin stitch.

       that's not for the rhyme just a thought at night time."
leader: "yeah just as nocturnal as criminal. offence as act of

       defence. not for the rhythm. just a wet dream."
madame: "ha you missed that one."
leader: "yeah hissed and won like the snake at the lake."
madame: "did a double-take"
leader: "rubble at the stake"
madame: "no just trouble on the make"
leader: "shake the marble"
madame: "when you wake with a bubble"
leader: "tumble with me let's bake"
(exit with a legit rake of each the other's thimble.
the leader and his transvestite with mirage image sans dent.
screaming relent or i'll have you sent to the movement
without a mauve cent. blah blah ha ha ha!) an alcoholic
has been at it? it's blonde. the sacrificial lambs stink on the
dinner tables the queues lengthen outside toilets everybody
needs to get the shit out but it wants our vote. & it will get it.
whether you're in agreement or not. 'cos shit is power.

i got out of it & walked. the machinery dipped into pulsing
brains. the steel shining in memory. the whitewash floating
on top of filth the sickness of mornings within mornings
within... caught up in the spirals of comings laughing &
goings of whorish tones in angel dress. doctors & mind
technicians. hate days the ammonia days the ether heads
the screaming the grinning the mucus on the walls. the
callouses dripping dirt. the steaming madness. i got out of it
& walked into the mist. the morning traffic rattles electrodes
in some sadist's terror story wrapped around characters out
of a cobwebbed cartoon book. the cold ground rose with

my step & hit me on the head. out of town i felt i wanted
to touch vomit to retch into my mouth swirl it within inhale
it deep & feel the cleansing touch purity. the rain started to
drizzle. i walked going nowhere. a wild feeling behind some
mouthwashed sanity walls. "don't go near the inmates who
knows what madness depths they might drag you into…"
the man mad streets screeched around kicking dust laughing
into the distance where i went wilderness walking knowing
nothing about where it was. the gates earlier on clanged shut
on mouth screaming wild countless days of subversion of
values hunt & counter-hunt & lines thrown out. "make believe
you're mad… hold on the thread is going comrade just a few
more months while we tie things up." my mind was tied up
but the time arrived so the gates clanged behind me where
i started going nowhere. the soup bile food washed down
with urine or smashed foetuses & dog blood plus cat brain
for dessert i retched & merciless nothing came up. i had the
paper tearing at the seams in the heat of my pocket some
change & a pack of cigarettes. my inventory done i hitched
the wrinkled time bag onto my back & crawled into the snail
traffic approaching midday.

"you're very intelligent bavino bashana you'll pull through…"
the whitecoat & grey eyes told me & gave me a kiss on the
forehead handed me the bag & rushed in when i saw the
tears welling in her eyes. & i stood for a while looking hard
at the whitewashed walls insane against the background
dirt mountain in the distance smoking old & creaking & i
walked into town. i refused the ride on the back of the van
white with a stripe of black new south african mad machine
rattling into the distance of nonsense & wanted to feel the
ground under my feet once more. ah tizzah, the papers
celebrate. martyrdom is blood on the tracks leaders walk on
extolling names riddled in the sand of history. labels in the
stars. we see them at night in our nightmares. us who walk
on the darkside of goo's glory. the near past was a time of
great festivity. "we drink our own blood to the names of our
heroes…"

they wrote tizzah's name in the capitals of the money stream

world. "died in the name of a first class just cause..." i walk
alone. look around to see if strange people are staring at
my own strangeness but no. the breeze takes a turn where
the road curves for the last lap. the city naps under cover
of smog doping itself. the noise pollutes false tranquillity
throbbing with my temples of doom. hooting cars are the
salute to my return but someone is doing a death dance on
the road & they're applauding them not me. the bag is heavy.
i'm crying. use my sleeve. not good for a grown man however
much fiction may have it. the rain-whipped dust whirls into
my mouth where i stare agape at a child scratching in the
dirt lifting filth to its mouth & the mother smiling thinking the
child very clever to have found a worm in this weather.

the drizzle comes down darting pins on the tar they hurry
away. what madness of the elements this. i walk on
getting wet. feel like jumping up hurraying. the walls have
left imprints imprisoning my mind. pinned there a load
of needles stabbing through my vision start lights on the
ceiling of my memory i close my eyes stagger into the road.
invective bounces me back. a screech passing by hurls
bricks shattering bottles on the pavement calling me some
anatomical part of some misbred animal. i stop. & grin when
someone rushing by laughs loud shrill through my stupor
"are you mad you little malformed testis?" raincoats to the
collar pass where i fall into step with society. the sleep jabs
my eyes. i'm always forgetting where i am. but here i am
now all round excesses surround me. there's cultured talk
here, educated & ambitious. there's the crushing weight
of the mass media. there are corporate tools on two legs.
walking around with antennae deep in the head. there's
metabolic malfunctions because there are magnetic tapes
& cameras deep in the human system. there's alcohol
floods & garbage heaps of great monetary value crawling
around in foreign made automobiles, drunkenness on too
much useless information & sex... sex... these are liberated
creatures in flatland existence. not debauchery so much as
a deep connection to too many horrors deadened senses &
selective memory, they key in to memory values & make tiny
withdrawals when the need arises. other than that they push

all reminiscence deep in some alimentary corner. these are
walking young adult terrors i might shake paws with raise
fore-legs in grudging greeting. making me feel like giving out

THE BABYLON MISSION REPORT. i shout it out in
silence running down the walls of my depths. still
it goes out to them. there's total transformation in
this babylon with a mission. man & nation caught
in stagnation. a total lunatic eclipse. unblock your
brain-pipes & bare the soul to sights of its own filth
now worms squirm on velvet cushions of a national
pshychosis. heroes of the aborted revolution. the poet
wrote shit & got a faeces deposit. they shat in his
mouth & when the rot stuck in his throat they thrust
a nail in it. got to the heart of the matter. the heroes
of the aborted revolution. this world is of starved
children. they got the glutton to set his appetite
straight strung him from a tree. by his intestines.
the heroes of the aborted revolution.
they impaled the wayward girl on a promiscuity
count. drove a stake up her vagina. counting it one
inch per penis / cock she'd had. & at the end of it
the wood pierced through her skull. "look how she
walks" they laughed & joked about "bitches
stretched cunts & bandy legs". the heroes of the
aborted revolution. along the dead way this man
went astray. shed his parental responsibility. they
relieved him of his load. with impunity built a fire
around his genitals & called him "balls of flame".
& when the testes exploded the people applauded.
cracked champagne in their minds. laughed &
puffed smoke to a stupor. as his seed spurted
between his legs in grey vapour chanting impotence
they wriggled their hips & went away. the heroes
of the aborted revolution. for miscegenation, they
called it degeneration, the gods of pigment said this
man could only see white. needed to be shown the
light. get his sights set right. they poked his eyes
out. & the VOID stared. like a mouth scared. locked
in a silent scream / shout. lit gasoline got the eyes

burnt. & when the eyeballs popped charred black
applause all around they hopped about. the heroes
of the aborted revolution. judges of morality they
passed judgement guilty & death-row on a woman
pregnant they said "with contamination of a nation
in birth-throes". for the moral question they slashed
her stomach open. ripped out the foetus & ejaculated
in her bleeding hole. injections of purity. & for
"transgressions of the parent" as the bible statement
lays down they bashed the unformed skull in. "the
wages of sin" like for the prophet "is paid out in
a stone" by the heroes of the aborted revolution.
genesis to revelations. eternal hysteria. the present's
conflagration towards posterity's conception. negative
perception transmission for positive reception.
sanity's a bone society breaks its fangs on. locked in
hallucination. they walk now on the soles of a pay-off
for services rendered in the interests of the nation's
birth. they're dawn's midwife generation. which is
mine. & it beats against the walls of my SMALL
ROOM OF UNFORMED MIND.
i'm caught in the teeth of madness. boiled in
the crucible of mass hysteria. kicked awake in
invocations of the green banknoted fire. ecstatic
cackles of the golden egg laid on shit tables. there
were twelve dwarves squeaking at last suppers.
fire denunciations of ice. peace crimes of war's
motivation. feel like i'm hanged by the neck in
climaxes of emotion. convexations of flesh & spirit.
i give attention to the dead in the fire. of commerce
incendiary. popping eye tumescence of sleep in the
walking stream of time. dreams in nightmare street.
the assertion of the will to being. water dizzied at
steam height. conflicts ossified in ice lay claim to the
tumult of infernos volcanoes. restless. there's poetic
intensity in outspoken chroniclers of the time resident
in backwaters of silence. in the head. tremors of the
earth in hearts pounding terrors in revelations of our
frenzy. transience in earth-whipped winds /minds.
this is an embryo murder initiation.

i move between word & sword into the wordsword.
surrounded by blockheads fiery mad speaking only when
ignited by the matches of economics. they rent a guerilla
squad. cosmic essences the deflowering of innocent talk on
the anvil of enlightenment. maidenhead decapitation on the
altar of debauchery. drums of labour in pain birthing children
of the lie. the warped image. souls bottled in wombs of
stone. i stare into broken mirrors of the future. search for the
continuation of the deception? is it gunshots put respect on
the boards? when a gunman walks in all heads bow to the
god of the moment. beyond the apocalypse walk, past the
boards of ashen dreams, hallucinating the flood of polluted
mindstreams on the flesh of thought bitten to a death-grin,
the life fluid flows. & it's mean cold & later than mere rage
sitting on a live-wire in blackness against whiteness. later
than broken glass of class war. it's illuminated in here, the
brightness of a mad world. have said before my colour comes
from compressed uterine heat. it's said all things converge &
merge at heartcore. i roll in the groove to get warm. enough
to sleep. in the embrace of dreams multilayered with the
reality that be. themselves that reality i shuffle the existence
code around. why did i get hooked up? i rolled in the dirt to
come out clean & it made sense. the man has come to collect
on my life. i'm getting out of the life system. my strength
is running to far corners from where i sit. trying to get out.
they shoot deserters in the army but well but are we an army
of one, my constitution & i? inside amputated limbs flutter
flailing in the wind. hysterical screaming creatures without
form sink fangs in my throat. can i choke in pensmoke? that's
a joke to take seriously. an arse-shifting tune with a classic
beat. hypnotic strains symphonic. enunciate the effect on my
tongue. purulent. lucidity. there are vivid spaces in my mind.
often lightning flashes & ugly sights are revealed naked. in
fever i sit shiver myself back to empty headedness. it's safe
in there. perspiration drops ruins the lines i define inscribe
on the flesh of the papersheet. the hiss gets out without
premeditation. dress my hysteria in steps i measure out in
streets.

there's a bar a while ago i used to go to. ah there. i walk
in. some see me recognition flames they pump my back &
say "man you well hey when did you get put out... heard
you were in the madhouse oh sorry didn't mean that here
have a beer..." the first in cracked throat months. i'm back
home. & now the madness begins. or resumes. within
my trendoid generation. cyber-spaced-out caught in some
electronic spiderweb. surfing in their own discharge. they
are little creatures trapped in the cages of their hyper-
electrified minds. nowhere to go but inside. desolate souls
on the sugarcandied low-way. all walking around with
earthshattering revelations in search of a congregation. but
ears all around the walls of conscience they pretend to have
killed. these are the super-live ones who killed not only god
but satan as well. thrust lucifer's horns through his throat &
choked him on his tail. they drive very concretely across the
bodies of all angels. alienated from all including themselves.
it's neglect no cosmetics can disguise. fuck it open all the
channels way beyond the five make hugo boss an underling
make calvin ever kleiner they are none of them a victim de
la mode except perhaps in living philosophy. yes they give
out ineffectual cries "we're organising a young intellectuals'
group..." the intellect crushes against my beer glass shatters
my thought so heavily doped it is. take your ideas sniff snort
or shove them up your veins. if that won't do try plugging
them up your arse. indeed the sex experiments won't stop
until not a muscle is left with any twitter of motion left in it.
all holes forever plug till death do us... yet they are lightning
intelligent but then only the thunder is left rolling way off into
the distance of their oblivion.

when the shot settles, they are grey. race is no issue
governmental or otherwise. but the greyness is in the
system of the lonely insecure zero level non-people with
names flaming in neon. but there's a fuse blown in that
machinery. the names are burnt to ash flutter down to the
dirt. where they stand surveying the tomorrow horizon. hardly
whimpering just spouting philosophy. they blurt out nonsense
trying to gauge my sanity weigh my senses on a scale of
their fucked-upness. it's a long way from home where i sit

amid red stenches, waters broken, old crumpled newspapers
wrung out with that spent life in them, torn sheets, plastic
washbasins & slopbuckets filled with little bits of bone &
flesh, synthetic because the acid would eat away the organic
& the doped screams animal howls pathic in the midnight
splintering light, the slit veins & little clits vibrating in the
electric wind, crawling up the wall with saggy old labia trying
hard to hold on tight though the elasticity is gone way far
away, & balls crushed under walls of haggardy tired walls
that couldn't take the strain of constant pounding anymore, &
the nausea & noxious flood of urine & faecal matter through
which i wade to the toilet & surprise a couple with eyeballs
hanging out dragging in that mire fucking & without shame
or embarrassment they adjust their pose to let me pass &
ask "wanna have some man?" with little naughty grins "no
thanks" & the girl giggles raising bubbles in that filth, &
someone throw out that abortion it's trying to hide inside my
flesh. it's a siege.

sitting down to shit i feel something scratching my buttocks
& jump up in fear look down to discover a rotting decapitated
infant head stuck inside the toilet bowl staring at my
nakedness. i slip & slide crashing out of there doing my
trousers up on the hoof & they laugh coming hysterical... i
rejoin their images. one of them rabbits out to get a poster
of quotes from review page clips suggests it as a book-cover
with the blurb hanging its tongue out licking. it's a burroughs
dream: "...has a morbid obsession with the human body...
inspires disgust with relentless mockings of the body's
biological functions... going blacker than bad... in contempt
of pomposity is that pompoxity... awing power burning rage...
radical... this is demonic possession... ferociously rooted
in both the astral & the wormlevel... rootical (yes i... live &
direct from me myself & irie ites... dread going out to you)...
shirks moralising with disdain... intellectual masturbation...
a profundity terrifying in its bleakness... mean man spirited
seen? abject complexity bursting all pretences open...
impotence the myths of patriarchs of the empty head...
repugnance spews forth from these pages of life & a death
that is... a sense of the spirit in flight simultaneously all so

flesh-based... comics the baseness of man & come to the
dick of it, the base woman... keen, taut... breaks itself on the
mild teeth indignance of immature rebellion..."
& then rejection slips. they yank out of tightened buttocks:
"thank you for showing us bavino bashana's work which,
although we were very impressed with his command of
language and writing talent, we must decline to publish. he is
a very promising writer indeed, but his staccato style & form
doesn't work for pieces much longer than the average poem.
it is just too difficult to follow and understand, too intense,
dense and with no sense of 'space'..."
"i enclose the samples of bavino bashana's poetry you kindly
sent us. as i explained, we do not feel it would be quite right
for our list but we greatly appreciated having the chance to
see it..."
stick your tongue up my arsehole. & i'll write a poem on
your soul. this is a new page in that chapter of life lived
with a knife between the eyes. platoons moving between
the letters. it's a mass of bodies & sounds, animal noises
pinning me down to my chair & i'm suffocating in that thick
liquid heat rising out from inside me. spinning away blown
off my senses' ground by the force of some many presences
in my present & past. they're trying to get inside my head but
there's no space in there anymore. & it becomes funny. ha ha
ha i roll around in the mire of my disgust.

THEY HUNG IT on the skull of grinning commerce.
bookshops libraries gone bankrupt on illiteracy.
there's no containment for my thoughts. anarchy reigns in my
dome. i can't fashion them cohesively. thus i'm incoherent to
myself. & here, where states of consciousness are irreversibly
altered, all the hate bouncing against the walls & finding
no outlet turns inward. some scattered drug induced atoms
rush about crashing from trembling lips into alcohol glasses
"hey mr leader don't fuck with my constitution... you taught
me to be rabid without order ungovernable... & i can't live
with peace... so i'm turning around one eighty degrees... to
fight the only enemy i can spot left... you. i want to believe
i defeated vanquished utterly destroyed... the rest. their
daughters ran to suck the oppression out of my cock..." but

it's said so low it doesn't even carry to the leader's image.
as regal on television & newspaper at the top of the human
stairs the leader emerges. a victor of unknown wars. all
human relations being based on deception the leader is
universally loved because he's the greatest con-man of all
time. bigger than jesus & the beatles. the script is brilliant.
he is well loved acclaimed worldwide they never cease to
paint his charisma. they said that about hitler.

alienation resides here. schizophrenia where dream &
reality walk down the street sit at bar table together get
drunk & mouth platitudes in the truth that be. shaping
crack baby consciousness. analysis rising in the stench
of diseased crotches drowned in expensive perfume. they
celebrate themselves as "internal exiles. irreconcilable. non-
participating..." lifting it from some book. eroded by hatred.
masochistic pains of nuns posing before cheap coffins of their
righteousness' purulent genitalia. where's the next generation?
not on the path of moral aid. they stand hearts' hands
outstretched to the i.m.f. & store their souls in the world
bank. they drag their hearts on spiritual crutches artificial legs
stumps of amputated limbs trembling in the laughing wind
to their little corners of the nation. orgasm-inducing. the talk
of crucified death believers. spare me "grace on the crusade"
it's all a thief of life. ma, they are trying to get at my seed
to define the me in "little cretin" dip pens in semen hunt out
my sperm fine i'm vermin. venom beyond the skies of what
criticism? but what grey matters? nothing of any importance
only in the minds of abortions. the blows storm down lips
ripe melon split open eyes gouged out steel descends on the
head cut to crimson sun sights. lead in the stomach ah...
ah... they try to move bowels in toilets full of constipation.
there's diarrhoea of the mind. ease out the abstraction
phrase the meaning beyond the silence of dead lines & the
schizophrenic gets frantic on the single track. the nod in
any direction is no affirmation coming from the paranoid.
layers lay down folds form. but within scabs the low down
creeping. perfumed in their own dung. the light goes down
where the night glows red. the sequel seeks to maintain
the original value. but before the blood dries the flames rise

& another human dies stressed out in doubt pressed hard
against the screamwall. it's divine salvation time eat what
you excrete the ultimate treat thrown down in proclamation
from the leader's table. blessed is the seed & righteous the
meaning beyond the heartbeat but no life beyond the mind.
into the pit. define the barriers in hell amid dead screaming
embryos. at the primeval crossroads. blindness lurks not
in darkness' alleyways it lives in the hills of righteousness.
remember the calvary sun on the seed sown in flood. blood.
visions drowned in sweat of daylight. mesh tangled visions
of human souls on the burn. where alien design doctrines
are drummed into the conscious born of the horn of man one
step before creation. in flame union of melting metal & leaden
water. on the throne of the one pierced in the side died so
tickled couldn't stop laughing until three days later fellated
to a gurgling resurrection. thus fueled hurtled flown drawn
into the dark heavenside. head puppet on a bloodstring. such
creatures of mythology a burden on the mind of man true or
false taught feeling & pain.

pull apart the statement cut between the lines for the real
shriek of sense said tattered nerves beat down to hysteria.
"the leader made the pillars shudder with mere force of
thundervoice..." the press crew tremble in awe though what
he said was pure nonsense. expressions of recognition's
sweat in the place where a dead sun-religion was revealed in
blood drip down to dust otherside of the street going nowhere
but down. describe a circumference around the senses &
stormswept fragments of mind stone the darkness. emotional
intensities insult to acted out realities. stir the galaxies for
emotion physically manifest. knowledge soul & the will's
bloody footprints. anger of a barren culture's existence on
nothing penitent in metalsounds making screams... a rush of
flame. green flames of the gloom hold the sky. worms slink
through rotted noses. in the charnel house of power tongs
clench around genitals. the word is out medical treatment is
a form of capital punishment. enter hospital at own peril as
breasts walk atrophying phalluses self-amputating at the root.

this is a state of morality. the leader's. & his religious values.
concentrated electricity loads hit the nerve centres explode
in the central lobes of the nation's brains. bloodstream
out. electromagnetic fields mapped out spinning around
in the metal heads of all in the medical corps. on the
sly the sycophantic are shipped out to healthier climes.
back here self-destruct biological still stand disinfectant
expectant. admittance in health centres is lethal. "today in
a press conference the health minister further stressed the
importance of health to the nation." sighs the deadbrained
newsreader on the television set above the bar & the beer
trembling in agitation. & that's the extent of the coverage.
babies are drowned in the mire of their own excrement.
many have died rolling around in their own vomit. while
the parents looked on. just. what is known is mere shadow
without truth's substance on putrefied lips. no life matter.
shadows recede fall apart reform in the distant gloom. but it's
all within. disembodied commands of the leader crash out of
craters in all buildings houses toilets schools no place is left
out. craters all around yawn. DO NOT PANIC THE LEADER
LOVES YOU. WILL PROVIDE. like marx. to them too busy
drumming the nails of dead ideology in the heads of the
hungry instead of providing hints on how to eke out some
existence out of the little living earth. allah willing. well he's
not. nat zach says he's too old. fumbling around searching
for his spectacles. to find them broken in the trampling feet
of the jihad. jehovah. died of a heart attack when the holy
mother sucked him off. the crockish heart couldn't take the
strain. all logic lost. inherent violence of the damned. brains
in labour birth the noise of chains dragged across concrete.
destruction is unleashed holds the head of the state of
infirmity across the sick psychoscape. fears throttled at birth
hang in the heavy broken wind of their own peace accord.
there's suffocation in whistles of bones grating against metal.
smoke sings a deathsong in the streets of summer whiteness.
there's deepseated restlessness in the nation. beyond the
surface smiles & ululations greeting the leader. "as attacks
on citizens increase at an alarming rate…" crackles through.
leaden. static.

beyond all screams there is silence. in the sewers & dumps scavenging humans have a feast of flesh. i feel stilted sensitivity of skin ligament muscle tissue ripped through. barricades of flame are wasps behind my eyelids. dust of century long crawl to here blocks my ducts. still tears chug heavy. muddied. down the years & the land of my face. as around me members of the "now" generation sink their talk to adolescent-boys-in-the-high-school-toilet-time:

"i thought you were on a black conscious trip... so why do you fuck white?"

"so i can see where my dick is going. i mean bonking black i might as well stick my cock in a hole in the ground... in any case black consciousness ends at waist level..."

& the walls show cracks in the laughter. & across the sex divide their sisters get non-sexist "he's always talking cum through his teeth everytime he sees me so i asked him why do you jerk at just mere sight of me you miserable little dick & he said 'cos you look just like a cunt..." & across the otherway of the sexes. "man she was so fat i had to wade through so many folds that... i mean i remember a point where i had just shifted a particularly huge mountain of lipids & balanced it on my shoulder & was trying to reach for the next level... & all the while i could feel it pushing bearing down on my back crushing against my bones it was such a struggle all that load at the back of my neck man pulling me down my muscles gave in & i fell headfirst into the heart of things... that's something a bit like a dam drying in there you know... a little mucky?... with fish thrashing about in there gasping for a last breath down there... but you know man that's about when my dick was talking to me at its loudest telling me things & threatening to rip itself up & that's a fate worse than... anyway so with a loud squelch i bunch my muscles... see you can tell how i've developed massive biceps from all exercise so i pulled pumped & pushed against all that massive flesh but i opened my eyes wide when i saw what lay within... man i passed out for a second & woke up with my face deep in that watery hole & she let me wallow in there for a while but by & by she lifted me out pretty much like an adult toy a blow-up doll like they sell in those places the concerned moral-custodians are trying to close down...

well anyway that's how my nose got so squashed it must have happened when i landed in there…" before he finished his anecdote with an adolescent giggle a particularly huge woman who'd been sitting off to the side taking up enough space for three rose up breaking sweat rising up with the sound of chairs screaming in relief waddled over to him & the sight of triceps vibrating with a ripple a rise & a fall that made me shut my eyes for a while she took an almighty backhanded wack at his face. sending him sliding across the room on his nose. when that dust settles off to another corner is the sight of a rainbow new man couple & the sound of them talking.

he says: "what do you mean i'm the ultimate stereotype buster black man…"
she: "well i've seen you dance around trying to take a piss & bring a torch along so that you can manage to find your dick in the dark it's so small…"
"well you know am i to blame that you're bigger than that fucking swimming pool your parents have… jesus fucking h. (whatever that stands for) christ… i mean there's no way i can park my dick in your bus depot…"
she responds with a hormone dripping smile: "yeah but that's a bigger statement than the truth & you don't know the half of it… i mean i struggle to find it under the burning sun let alone a flashlight… i actually wonder if you've ever seen your own cock…"
"fuck you…"
"no you can't man remember you don't even lean towards the walls let alone touch them…" they say lots & all the while the place expands in laughter as he visibly shrinks in size.

symbolic of the rainbow's end when the sun comes up. but it bubbles up in my glass. riots around my belly. will it rise in storm stern foul temper with a raised fist come crushing out of my mouth to scrawl vile messages on the floor? that was in my past & lives with me still. i keep vomiting. but these days its mostly in words. & that's what's a problem for the land cloaked in novelty. it wants its surfaces gleaming. polished. even if by human life-fluid. nothing is filthy here.

in the minds of the new people & that's what a new nation needs. guiltlessness. so they've all killed theirs. reinvented their own jesus to die for their sins & absolve them. heavy titted & bearded babies of the new order. but the smell of cannibalism hangs red & liquid in the air.

i puke deep inside my head. it spins around in there. is bound to come spilling out soon. i shove it down & sit on it. it pushes against my memory banks. & that constipates my tongue. burning spear said it's dry & heavy & that's how it is where my vocal chords live. & still the drinks go down. all around. that oil is wasted on my machinery. they keep vulturously looking at me. they are on a hunt. predators. feel like i'm wriggling around on a plate while knives get sharpened all around me. the blade glints they keep pushing my head under the guillotine. want me to say what they've been programmed to hear from me so they can proceed to feed. but everything i want to express is glued in there deep within. won't show its face its buttocks won't come flashing out. it remains dark & cold inside. no fires flare. so other areas of wet interest light themselves up. heated. moisture holds the space. they're pushing the bait deep down my throat. & then it's freeing expression time. as the script dictates. "you see these censors are just selfish old jerks. imagine a guy spending everyday goggling tits & bums & cocks & cunts all day & then poking a semen dripping finger at it until it's glue sticking to the pages deciding no this movie or this book or this photograph is too good it makes you come quickly it shouldn't be viewed by the masses... custodians of morals all of them walking around waving biceps all knotted with too much pulling & pumping when they masturbate..." another: "the political sphere is business enterprise. the money machines are crippled in chambers of commerce."

sad
snarled days machinery system
people living in damnable urgency
oppressors enjoying prevalence on sanity fruits
the seed over robed decency
democracy on trial desecrated in grave moments
rotten organisational talk
stunted growth moss covered tongues
the fire professes saintliness
courting society's death's special purpose corpse
sad
brothers' keepers powerhouse melancholy
bilious in sacresy
putrescine constitutional bumbling/humbling
on the block of tyranny's sculleries
scallywog/sally the wog poetry
it's sad
i have tied my arms to senile descent's rock
cut to tottering sickness size
sad
jail wise birds twitter electrical wings
heaping afloat above jungle fire floods
ponderous make believe games
reaching brains turned inward astronomical heights
warding off madness' tentacles turned in on jumbled thoughts
memories things that never were nor will be flying in the
wind
paper thoughts
sad
up the windstreet
jesus ghosts howling licking debrained pasts' brains
mentalities beating filth presents over the head
with the southern star
turning a blind eyeball in the dust
sad
oil tanks greasing desert hopes firing the desert's creaky
bones
moving on kuwait iran resplendent in golden liquid glory
burning in the sun
sad

tomorrow iraq's alphabetical dictation fast typing machine
guns
writing terrorsounds' anatomy in discourse's throat
in god / allah's midday eye
we like a.k. bared
sad
deathscrews in oil & gun barrels zooming in on tv screens
tumbling from radios' cat whiskers purring boot-tongues
licking
droppings off crumb tables
sad
brains bursting to litter
glass is the jagged way out of the morass
flailing pieces in the air
hair in the wind broken under the jackboot
life's death-maze
sneering moustaches hold red dripping hands
sad
generals walking free

the leader has checked into a rejuvenation centre. age
besieged cardiac valves are massaged by machine. doctors &
nurses operate under the snout of the gun-barrel. even there
though, the bodies multiply on the leather couches become
mortuary slabs. but somewhere here stethoscopes in stealth
poise in hangman fashion. here & there syringes stick out
of necks. are stilettos on both sides of the operating table.
"grotesque dealings out of health." a word glut ventures. the
talk spins around ever whirling with the spiralling smoke &
i feel my senses grow sleepy-eye heavy. i raise my glass to
the health of the leader. for life. where he lays down the law
to die. house calls & kissing of babies with one grown eye
on the video cameras. as the shutters fall so the wrinkled
phallus under attack from senility rises. someone must have
dropped a dead load on my head. i'm groggy sensed. the
television's sound goes honeyed. & it kills. it's a police file
set to sharpen perceptions. but still i'm dulled. "we interrupt
this..." seeps oily through the concrete of my descent. all
around the inspired talk drops dead. as the rand land's
currency devaluates going down with me the leader's face

rises & shines in value on the mass' media screen with fat
glowing from deep within the slits in the wrinkles where
that rock of the age (or is it the ages?) is cracked & eroded.
"disturbed... might be dressed up in the drag of a poet...
making rabid statements... defending certain values that he's
not making quite clear... clear sign of subversion..." it flows
on. on the smooth wheels of charisma's polish. pulls to a
stop on: "...intercept!"

i turn my head warward fingers inching towards the first
mental bomb. aimed to drop on his genitals. but i find my
hand trembling against the glass. of my mind. lifting not
my hand but the weight of my eyes. & they are all around
me. they've closed me in. grabbing. digging. their talk had
chloroformed my senses to false peace. tranquil spaces.
lapses. & there's nowhere to run. not even inside myself
because they're already there. occupying my head. still
reaching down. & deep. & beyond my last thought: i'm worse
than god. they haven't allowed me even one full day of rest.
no sabbath day for the wicked. & mama i'm scared...

johannesburg 1992 - stuttgart 1997